WAITING FOR TEN

WAITING FOR TEN

A NOVELLA

JASON W PARK, PhD

J.J. MAGIK
— publishing —

Trade paperback ISBN: 978-1-7366662-2-7; Kindle 978-1-7366662-3-4; EPUB 978-1-7366662-4-1

Library of Congress Catalog Number: 2026903820

Editors: Robin Quinn, Gerald Everett Jones

Copyediting and book design: La Puerta Productions

Cover images: Shutterstock and Canva Pro

Author photo: Mr. Yuno Cho and Studio Q Photography

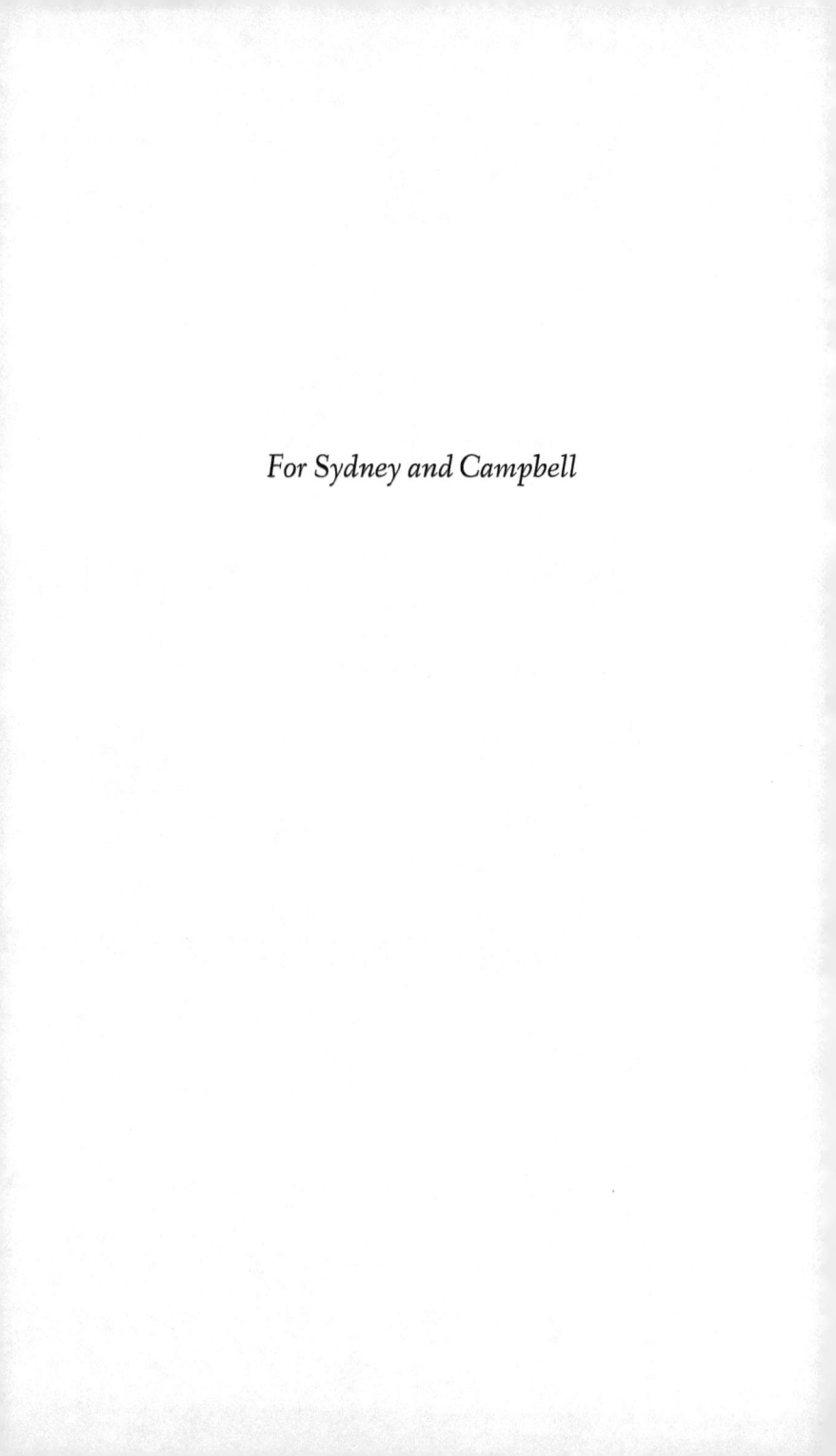

For Sydney and Campbell

OCTOBER

DOWN THE RABBIT HOLE

OCTOBER - WEEK 1

Bam, bam, bam! Uncle Frank pounded on the door to the guest room. "Skyler, turn the music down!"

Oomph, oomph, oomph! The house music on DJ Dan's album *Beats for Freaks* featuring the track "Visions of the Future (DJ Skull Remix)" by Gene Farris hammered away from the other side of the door.

Urgent. Frenetic. Up-tempo. Beautiful.

"Skyler, can you hear me?"

Oomph, oomph, oomph! More hammering away.

BAM, BAM, BAM! "Skyler, turn the noise down now!"

Suddenly, there was silence. Then in its place drifted Italian Baroque music: "Diverse bizzarie sopra la Vecchia Sarabanda ò pur Ciaccona (Various

Caprices on the Old Sarabande or Chaconne)" by Nicola Matteis, performed by the Palladian Ensemble.

Brilliant. Stately. Poised. Gorgeous.

"Skyler, your aunt and I have had enough. Open the door right this second."

The bolt-action lock on the door slid and released, and Skyler opened the door a crack.

"Let me in, Skyler. I want to talk to you." Uncle Frank's voice softened from angry to concerned.

Skyler flew the door wide open, then slammed it closed unceremoniously in Uncle Frank's face. Sputtering, Skyler's uncle then forced the door open by himself and made his way to the only place in the room to sit, the bench that went with the pricey electronic keyboard, the young man's pride and joy. There stood Skyler in the center of the room, buck naked, clutching his sister Emily's "raver lid." It was a tubular cut of wool, colored playfully with purple and yellow stripes, and worn on the head on one open end, tied closed on the other with a string that dangled freely. Skyler quietly wept into the lid, while moaning in grief, "Emily, Emily, Emily — "

Skyler and Emily were playing checkers one night when their parents were away. "King me!" Emily squealed with joy as she handed Skyler defeat on a silver platter.

Unperturbed, Skyler imperiously declared to his kid sister, "Very well. Now then, it's time to play chess. But you don't know how to play, do you?"

Hushed, Emily declared, "Teach me, big brother. Checkers is too easy for me now!"

━━━

"Do you know what you did?" Uncle Frank's yell cut through Skyler's brain fog. "Look at all the disgusting graffiti everywhere. Walls, windows, floor, ceiling. Where did you get all that spray paint? This looks like a deserted New York City subway car, not a decent and respectable bedroom in Los Angeles. You had better clean this mess up. You have been screaming all night long! And where are your clothes? Do you know, in the middle of the night, you woke me and Aunt Nancy up when you walked in the backyard completely naked, tripping the flood nights, and screaming, 'You're not real!' over and over again? By the way, the neighbors complained, and I have to admit, they have a point."

"Hey, the devil made me do it, and I'm the devil. Okay?" Skyler's face displayed a deep, perplexed frown. But deep inside, he mulled over his rendezvous with the UCLA drug-dealer Reggie for the previous night's drug hookup for what Skyler thought was cocaine.

Damn! That didn't seem like cocaine at all. More like angel dust. That Reggie!

"Listen, you," Uncle Frank again broke into Skyler's train of thought. "Take this business card and call Ms. Eleanor Martinez to confirm your appointment for this morning at ten. She will call Dr. Ralph Wilson and coordinate with him to see you, back-to-back, at eleven. Remember those two?"

Eleanor and Ralph had been not only Skyler's therapist and psychiatrist, but they had also treated his late sister Emily. However, in the moment, it was convenient for Skyler to pretend he had no need of their help.

"Yeah, and a lot of good it did her." Skyler felt the hair on his neck stand on end, his whole body start to tremble, his palms turn sweaty, and his pulse begin to climb.

"Close your mouth! We're not going through this

again as a family like with Emily. If you don't call Ms. Martinez in the next fifteen minutes, I'll have you involuntarily committed. You don't want that to happen now, do you?"

"All right, all right! I'll call her!"

Uncle Frank ran his fingers through his hair in exasperation. He stood up and put a reassuring hand on Skyler's shoulder. "And by the way, if you think I'm being hard on you, remember that I just co-leased a very nice one-bedroom, furnished apartment for you in West Hollywood. There you will be the same distance to me and your Aunt Nancy in the Hollywood Hills, and just as close to Eleanor Martinez and Dr. Ralph Wilson in Larchmont Village. Later on, you can do sessions remotely with them. But for the first one, I want you to meet in person.

"There's plenty of space in your new apartment for your clothes, your keyboard, your CDs and your CD mixer. I want you to move out tonight, after you come back from Larchmont Village. Here's the key fob for your new building's front door, and the key for your apartment door. I secured a parking space for your car too. Go to the leasing office by five-thirty this afternoon, co-sign the lease for your landlord Olga, and pay for the first and last month's rent. Also pay for the parking space."

"Why? I didn't do anything!"

Uncle Frank massaged his furrowed brow with one hand. "Your behavior has become more outrageous and bizarre ever since you graduated from UCLA. You terrified Aunt Nancy. You disrespected me. That's why we're sending you to therapy. You need more help than we can give you. Professional help."

"All right, Uncle Frank. There's nothing wrong with me, but since you're being an asshole and dangling involuntary commitment over my head, I'll go. It's not fair, because I'm just expressing myself. *Des Künstlers Gefühl ist sein Gesetz!* (The artist's feeling is his law!) But I'll still go."

"Whatever fairness means to you, Skyler, I'm still your uncle, and I still have your best interest at heart. And this is definitely who you are *not*. Your only concern must be to get yourself over to those sessions. They've been waiting for you. You have an hour and a half to get there. Now, get moving."

In the morning of that same day, Skyler drove from his uncle and aunt's place in the Hollywood Hills in his BMW 325i convertible. He sought moral support for his upcoming appointment in the music he chose to blare on the stereo.

It was time for a heavy-duty dose of Sergei Rachmaninoff's second piano concerto, performed by the Soviet Russian pianist Sviatoslav Richter. Skyler's love for classical music was especially acute because the great music drowned out (albeit temporarily) all the evil in the world.

If people truly knew what music meant to Skyler, they would think he was truly gifted. In a music appreciation class at UCLA, some of the pithier observations he could think of to impress his professor were, first of all: "Music is neither silence nor noise." At its most basic and fundamental level, this was Skyler's definition of music. It had a grammar, vocabulary, syntax, and even its own punctation. Second, "Music is a language without words." That was of course true for instrumental music, without accompaniment by a singer or a choir. And third, it occurred to Skyler that, in the case of music with vocals, "The music soothes the moods, while the lyrics speak to the soul." As in popular music, the catchy tune and smart sayings made for a winning formula. For Skyler, everything from Bach to Led Zeppelin and back was fair game for awesome music.

But pithy sayings alone were not Skyler's musical forte. From kindergarten through high school, he had spent close to ten thousand hours on piano instruction with an ambitious instructor who encouraged in Skyler a keen desire to excel. Five thousand hours of practice made one proficient at that activity. But ten thousand hours of practice made for mastery of it. He even managed to perform at New York City's Carnegie Hall as a youth in a solo piano recital with other young talented people. That achievement was Skyler's crowning glory in high school, even rivaling his acceptance to UCLA. Just the fact that he did it stunned his teachers and silenced his critics who said he would never make it there. Even he could not believe at times what he had accomplished. But practice was required, more practice than he ever thought possible. How do you play in Carnegie Hall? Practice, practice, practice! He spent more time in front of the family's Steinway piano than he did poring over chemistry textbooks or slaving away over calculus assignments.

Skyler's was one of those rare talents who could write about music and also perform it. That was why music was so all-encompassing to him. Most music programs at universities and colleges combined both activities, unlike conservatories such as Juilliard in New York or Colburn in Los Angeles, which focused solely on music as a performance art. UCLA played to Skyler's strengths by making him a more well-rounded individual and a more competitive candidate in the job market. But, ah, there was post-graduation from UCLA, when the shit hit the fan. The loss of his family combined with the symptoms of his diagnosis hit him hard.

It took over a half-hour to listen to the entire Rachmaninoff concerto, interpreted maturely and with awe-inspiring technique by Richter. Music therapy, indeed! This piece was in a sentiment of profound pathos that only that dour, late romantic Russian composer could make so uplifting, breathing into Skyler the will to "go on." Rachmaninoff had dedicated this concerto to Dr. Dahl, whose hypnotherapy had lifted the composer from a deep, extended depression. Music in this form was a pure, unadulterated joy, a form of treatment that neither talk therapy nor psychotropic medication could surpass.

As for his destination, Skyler knew where to go — a posh section of a high-rise office building in downtown Larchmont Village. Skyler knew this place well. His sister Emily had the same treatment team for her major depressive disorder. But before he left his car, he put on Emily's raver lid, her keepsake. In their high school years, she had always worn it to old-school "raves." Those were all-night dance parties in abandoned warehouses or out in the desert, with loudspeakers playing underground house and techno music, and with copious amounts of illicit drugs.

Emily had died, along with their mother and father, in a car accident. She was driving. Before they had departed from home for a dinner party, she was distraught and crying uncontrollably. On the road, she drifted over the center double-yellow line, and when a car coming the other direction collided at full-speed, the head-on impact destroyed all chances of survival. This happened last year, when Skyler was a twenty-year-old junior studying music performance at UCLA. He lucked out with a test he had to stay home and study for. But he did not feel lucky. He felt spared. And that feeling made him wonder if he was cursed with mental illness too. His family's tombstones sat to the side of Sunset Boulevard, just north of the Westwood campus, but after graduation Skyler stopped visiting the cemetery. It was too painful to go back and relive old memories — survivor's guilt. But that was all he had to go on — memories. It was still important to remember what they stood for and the values they had shared, even after their deaths. After all, they were not really dead so long as he remembered them. In fact, he suffered the most out of any in the family. He blamed himself for his family's deaths. Maybe he could have driven that night and left Emily at home to recover from her moods. Hypothetical scenarios abounded. It did drive him insane. It was an issue he needed to work on.

He looked at the roster in the lobby. Ms. Martinez's office was on the twelfth floor, while Dr. Wilson's office was on the tenth floor. "Very convenient, I guess..." Skyler growled out loud, turning heads as folks piled into the elevator. As it went up, he screamed, "It's my twelfth birthday!" at the top of his lungs as he reached the twelfth floor. But it wasn't. Alarm filled the faces in the elevator. Those getting off on the tenth floor hurried past him. The few that were left inside cowered in fear until the elevator door closed in front of them. Then they breathed a collective sigh of relief as Skyler exited the elevator on the twelfth floor.

In the waiting room, Skyler screamed, "I must see the doctor now!" then violently rattled the sliding glass window behind which the receptionist sat. Eleanor Martinez, a licensed clinical social worker, hurriedly opened a separate door to her office and motioned Skyler in.

She directed him to take a spot on a comfy cushioned couch, while she sat in an elegant, upholstered leather chair. She knew about Skyler's situation, although not necessarily his diagnosis — his family tragedy, level of educational achievement, and various life stressors. She knew him, yes, but mostly through Emily, so Eleanor needed more information to arrive at a proper diagnosis.

"Can you tell me why you're here, Skyler?"

"I don't fucking know. My uncle told me to come here. But nothing's wrong, I'm completely fine."

"Your uncle told me you screamed all sorts of gibberish, took off all your clothes, and ran around naked, spray-painted your whole room, claimed that someone was not real..."

"The voices told me to do it."

She scribbled on a notepad.

"So, you're having hallucinations? Hearing

things that aren't there? Do you see things that are not there too?"

"I don't hallucinate. I just hear things that other people don't hear."

More scribbling.

"Let's talk about your family. Your mom, dad, and Emily."

"Yeah, what about 'em?" Skyler snarled.

"I want to ask you how you feel about their —"

"You have no right to talk to me this way. You have absolutely no right to talk to me this way! Who do you think you are? Who the fuck do you think you are? You've really gotten to me this time. Do you understand? You really got to me this time. Fuck you!"

"Okay, Skyler, you've made your point," Ms. Martinez countered forcefully and with a glum scowl on her face. She had dealt with difficult patients in the past, and Emily had been one of them. It came with the territory, especially involving family therapy. "I want you to go see Dr. Wilson now. Suite 1004. You know the one?"

"Yeah, I do. I went there for my sister's family sessions. Now you can leave me alone."

"All right, go."

Skyler slammed the door shut behind him as he

left. Totally unfazed and dead serious, Ms. Martinez dialed a number. "Hi, Ralph. I just met with Skyler. So, I believe based on my assessment..."

━━━

Skyler descended to the tenth floor, heading to Dr. Wilson's office. He felt hot flashes and cold chills alternatively, as if he were being electrocuted. He heard voices that others do not hear.

Why don't you shoot yourself in the head? At least we could save the time and cost of a trial.

He shook his head violently in complete discomfort.

The doctor greeted him amiably. Skyler ignored the greeting and marched into the office as if it were his. He reclined on the leather-cushioned chair as if it were his throne. Wilson still maintained a professional demeanor, despite Skyler's childish arrogance, and sat in his own upholstered chair.

Wilson smiled. "Skyler, can you tell me why you're here?"

"I'm here because your reality is merely a perception. So, fuck you," Skyler hissed.

"Why would our realities be different?" The doctor reclined in his chair.

"Because I am the head of the family." Skyler shifted in his seat as if he could not sit still.

"Not Uncle Frank?" Dr. Wilson inquired comfortably.

"He can lie rotting and stinking in the earth, for all I care." Skyler shifted up and down in his seat.

"I'm sorry you feel that way. How *do* you feel?" Dr. Wilson calmly asked.

"I wish I knew."

"Does it have to do with your family that you lost?"

"Stop talking about my family!" Skyler started crying. Then the crying was abruptly replaced by a look of terror in his eyes. He exclaimed, "Oh, no! They're coming after me!" His eyes darted wildly around the doctor's office as he looked for the origins of such terror. He heard screams that nobody else could hear, along with the *chik-chik* of a shotgun with one in the chamber.

"Who are you talking about?" Dr. Wilson's curiosity was piqued. He knit his brows.

"They're here!" Skyler put his head in his hands. Sobbing, he fell apart.

"Who? Where?"

"The voices! They're talking to me!"

"What do they say, Skyler?"

"They're saying things like, 'You're worthless and you should kill yourself!'"

Dr. Wilson stated, "Okay, Skyler, I want you to wait here for a second."

He returned with Ms. Martinez, who sat down in another chair next to the doctor, both of them facing Skyler.

Dr. Wilson began, "We think we have a possible diagnosis for you — schizoaffective disorder. Now, it could be something else, like bipolar disorder with psychotic features. But the symptoms are very close, and the treatment approach would be very close too."

"Schizoaffective. What's that?" Suddenly, Skyler picked up on something in a moment of clarity.

Martinez stated, "It is a combination of a thought disorder and mood disorder. In your case, the mood disorder is bipolar type one. That's when you go very high up and very low down emotionally. The first one is mania, and the second one is depression. And then, in your case, the thought order manifests itself in auditory hallucinations, like the voices you hear that aren't there."

"So, what do I have to do? Do I have to take medication?" Skyler asked incredulously.

"Yes. And I will be seeing you for talk therapy once a week," Ms. Martinez told him.

"I have to do therapy, too?"

"Yes. Today's Friday so I will see you first thing Monday morning."

Skyler flailed away verbally, "I can't believe how stupid this is."

Ms. Martinez and Dr. Wilson conferred with each other. He told her, "For the bipolar, Depakote, two-fifty titrated up to five-hundred milligrams in two weeks. For the psychosis, Risperdal, from four titrated to eight milligrams per day in two weeks."

Martinez replied, "Two weeks at the low dosage, and two weeks on the full dosage..."

He nodded. "Correct."

He turned to Skyler. "Skyler, I have two prescriptions for you. Please go to your pharmacy and have them filled. Start taking them right away, tonight, before you go to bed. I will see you in one month."

Skyler grabbed the scripts from Dr. Wilson's outstretched hand and stormed out of the office without another word directed at his treatment team.

He had had enough. He was not planning on taking anything or talking about anything.

Returning to the Hollywood Hills to stop by his uncle and aunt's nearby pharmacy, Skyler found the whole process relatively unproblematic. He found that his curiosity was piqued by the prescriptions. He never had to take anything previously in his life. Now was he expected to follow a regimen of pills all his life and divulge his entire life story to a near-stranger?

Then, with his white paper bag in tow, Skyler returned to the privacy of his car and pulled out the two translucent orange-brown bottles:

Depakote Extended Release, 250 mg tablets. Take one tablet in the evening, with food, for 15 days. Then take 2 tablets in the evening, with food, for 15 days. Do NOT chew. Finish the whole bottle. Quantity 45. Refills: 0.

And the label on the other bottle said:

Risperdal 4 mg tablets. Take 1 tablet in the evening, with food, for 15 days. Then take 2 tablets in the evening, with food, for 15 days. Do NOT chew. Swallow whole. Finish the whole bottle. Quantity 45. Refills: 0.

As his therapists had explained, the Depakote, a mood stabilizer, was meant to smooth out Skyler's labile feelings, between depression and mania. Risperdal, an antipsychotic, was meant to quash the auditory hallucinations and Skyler's delusions. Apparently, both medications were sedating, hence the instructions to take them in the evening. And, despite what they had said, this was no quick fix. Dr. Wilson was taking no chances with the thirty-day amount — forty-five pills, no more, no less — in order to segue to a higher dosage for both medications after the initial two-week period. Skyler also suspected, with zero refills, the doctor intended to control how often Skyler needed to go to the pharmacy to get medication.

Oh, well, here goes nothing.

He turned on the stereo to the track "Have a Drink on Me" by the rock band AC/DC and listened to the self-effacing humor behind the lyrics. Not exactly the right attitude you would want to have with a new phase of one's life. Emily's major depressive disorder was diagnosed a few years ago, when she was placed on a medication regimen. She had celebrated her eighteenth birthday two weeks before the car crash and had been accepted to the College of William and Mary. He had overheard her expressing to their parents in the kitchen that she longed to be away from all the "gloom and doom" of the West Coast. The sun-drenched streets of Los Angeles were too "depressing" for her, while the cloudy, dreary winters in Williamsburg were just the "manic" atmosphere she needed. Apparently, a change in scenery and distance from home were all she needed to cure what ailed her.

Skyler returned the two bottles to the white paper bag and absent-mindedly tossed it in the passenger seat. He was curious about this "pad" in West Hollywood that Uncle Frank and Aunt Nancy had secured for him. Besides, now that he got kicked out of their house, he needed to be on his own for some time.

He drove up the winding streets of the Hollywood Hills until he saw the HOLLYWOOD sign high above and somewhat distant, at which point he pulled in the driveway to Uncle Frank and Aunt Nancy's contemporary glass-and-concrete habitat. Shutting the engine off, Skyler clambered up the steps with his prescriptions to the entrance and banged on the door.

———

Uncle Frank swung open the front entrance. "Hello, my nephew. Did you get those prescriptions filled, as Dr. Wilson asked you to?"

"How would you know?" Skyler shoved the crinkled white paper bag in Uncle Frank's face. He pulled out the two bottles and shook them violently up and down, an inch from Uncle Frank's nose. All full.

"I'll take the first dose tonight, before I go to bed. At my new pad."

Not reciprocating Skyler's gloomy negativity, Uncle Frank strained to reply amiably, "Good, Skyler. I'm very proud of you. You have taken your first step into the world of recovery."

"Uncle Frank, I need money! With this schizoaffective disorder, there is no way I can work."

"What? Have you lost your job?"

"No. But how am I going to support myself if I am mentally incapacitated?"

"Let's cross that bridge when we get there. As of now, I still expect you to work."

Although it was tough love, it was still out of compassion that Uncle Frank expressed it. He was covering for Skyler because he did not want him involuntarily committed. He still harbored the belief that his nephew could control himself in a workplace setting.

"Oh, fuck you!"

"Skyler, watch your language. Once you start making progress with the therapy and medication, then let's talk. Remember, I'm paying for your health insurance, which covers your doctors' visits and for the medications, and I'm co-leasing your new apartment, plus paying for your phone. Other than that, I'm not giving you anything more, not until you get better. Forget about any more money. I'm through with this discussion."

But Skyler had ten-thousand bucks in his bank account, just sitting there, begging to be put into action, all painstakingly accrued from his summer jobs, his allowance over the years, his campus job at one of the libraries at UCLA, and now from his first real job at Raleigh Studios, the entertainment company. "Well, where there's a will, there's a way," Skyler muttered in clear earshot of Uncle Frank.

"What's that?" Uncle Frank voiced his suspicion. Did Skyler have any other sources of income? But the moment passed, and then he returned to his casual, open demeanor. "Honestly, Skyler, let's worry about money when the time comes. Right now, it would be a waste if I gave you any money. You would spend it frivolously and fritter it all away."

"You don't fucking know that. Some uncle you are! Let me guess. My dad hated you."

Uncle Frank heaved a big sigh and said, "Quite the contrary, Skyler. He and I were very close, primarily because of you and Emily. And now, only because of you."

"Let's not bring Emily into this, okay?" Skyler snarled his discontent.

"Whatever you want."

Uncle Frank sighed again and returned to focus on more mundane matters. "Did you get all your stuff? I forgot to mention you have your laptop there on your desk. You'll want to bring that to your new place, for sure." Uncle Frank still looked out for Skyler, in the moment.

Skyler carried his personal possessions downstairs and into the passenger seat, into the backseats, and into the trunk of his convertible. His electronic keyboard was the hardest to stow away because of its eighty-eight key length and heavy, foot-long depth.

But ultimately, it did fit in the trunk. The CDs went in a box on the floor of the passenger-side backseat, and the CD mixer went on the floor of the driver-side backseat. The laptop went in a backpack on the passenger side front seat, for ease of access. He placed his phone between the two front seats and plugged it into a charger.

Finally, Skyler strewed the backseat with his clothes: two-dozen two- and three-piece suits, all meant for his management role at Raleigh Studios as Chief Science Officer. In other words, he directed a team to apply science to management problems, then to report their results to the Chief Executive Officer to provide an informed opinion on a course of action.

For Skyler, his dual degree at UCLA, one in science and one in the arts, informed each other. When physicists try to explain the world, they take all varied and large amounts of data and try to boil it down to a small number of equations — or even just one "elegant" equation. There is an aesthetic to the enterprise. And just as well, when musicians compose music, there has to be a pristine logic and sensibility to it that could only be called "scientific." Thus, in a sartorial vein, that was why Skyler was just as comfortable wearing Emily's lid on his head as he was wearing a three-piece suit on his body.

Uncle Frank walked out to Skyler, who was now standing on the driveway by his convertible. Skyler hopped in, turned the motor over, and blared the jazz standard "My Melancholy Baby" performed by trumpeter Dizzy Gillespie and saxophonist Charlie Parker on the stereo. The lines of the song fit the occasion: "Come to me, my melancholy baby / Cuddle up and don't be blue" and "Smile, my honey dear, while I kiss away each tear / Or else I shall be melancholy too." Skyler looked in the rearview mirror for oncoming traffic while backing out — all while ignoring Uncle Frank's farewell wave and vocal goodbyes.

Skyler headed south, one lonely and sad being leaving behind another lonely and sad being. If only Skyler had turned around in his seat and bothered to notice how careworn Uncle Frank's face was!

━━━

When Skyler got to West Hollywood for the first time to see his new pad, he could not tell from the outside what he was getting into. The garage gate opened robotically at the click of a button, sliding from right to left. No clues yet. Once in the garage, he looked for his space in the covered lot: A3. The spot was the easiest of all thirty to get into and out of, while the others required some rather awkward three-point parking.

He stopped by the apartment office to co-sign his lease in the presence of a smiling immigrant lady in her sixties who spoke English with a thick Eastern European accent. With Olga's help, he made the first and last month payments, four thousand dollars total, plus an additional twenty-five dollar deposit for the parking space.

Then he went up to Apartment 207 to see the new digs.

It was about eight hundred square feet: living room, separate kitchen, bedroom, separate bathroom — everything he needed. And, it was furnished with a leather three-seater, porcelain lamps, a wooden dining table, wooden cabinets, a TV, two sets of dinner plates, glasses, soup bowls, flatware sets, microwave, toaster, large refrigerator — again, everything he needed. And what else was not to like? A/C, heat, sliding windows overlooking a small, manicured lawn, a view of the rising sun, privacy provided by wooden blinds.

This is no dump. Uncle Frank and Aunt Nancy are looking out for me.

Satisfied with his new place, Skyler began the slow, excruciating process of lugging his possessions into the apartment. College had taught him to be patient and methodical when moving from place to place, but it never stopped getting old. He started with the keyboard and its stand, with both hands, not damaging the sensitive electronics inside the instrument. Then came the book of CDs and CD mixer, the latter being heavy despite its compact design, its weight being evidence of solid construction. Afterward, the two-dozen suits that had been custom-tailored for him. As a set of fabrics, the clothes might even serve as a makeshift mattress. Finally, the laptop and backpack with power cord that served as a conduit to the Internet. It still mattered to have a larger screen and a more comprehensive interface than a phone had, despite the latter's ubiquity.

He was able to do the transfer of his goods into his apartment without too much street-smart worry of burglary, since he saw no riffraff hanging around. The parking lot had a gate to it, and there were security cameras all around. But to Skyler, in his troubled state of mind, he could not be impressed by the quiet, stately opulence of it all. Even though his fraternity building at UCLA had been condemned just a few years back, Skyler could only think he deserved *better*. What he wanted and what he needed were two very different things. He willfully refused to be satisfied with his needs, and he could only be pacified by his wants. Discontent mired him in an aberrant mindset that could only be described as half-arrogance, half-entitlement. This pad could never reach his own unrealistically lofty standards. Maybe a penthouse in New York or a mansion in Malibu would serve him better.

Despite the bucolic peace he was surrounded by, intrusive thoughts kept coming in,

If you stabbed yourself dead, at least you would die with some honor still intact.

And then he remembered deeply about his family: he heard the rapping on the door, the police greeting him, notifying him of the deaths, his going to the station, the officers asking him to identify the bodies — Mom, Dad, Emily — the tidal wave of loss and grief smothering him.

Just then, his phone rang: 310-423-2433. He didn't recognize the number. But he picked up anyway.

"Hello?" Skyler sat down on the three-seater.

"Skyler? Is that you?" It was a friendly, sympathetic voice.

"Oh, hi Linda." Dread filled his body. It was his supervisor.

"Hey, the team missed you at work today. You didn't call in sick or show up. Is everything all right?"

Oh my God, now I'm screwed.

"Sorry, Linda, I felt sick as a dog, and I forgot to call in sick. I was just about to, even though it's already almost five o'clock. Sorry." His blood pressure inched upward.

"Oh, that's okay. We're kind of slow on things lately, so your absence didn't really affect things at the office much."

Whoa, that felt like a sly dig!

"Yeah, I'll be back in the saddle on Monday, for sure." Skyler hoped his fib would go undetected. "If anything pops up, let Barbara lead the team on the Paramount project."

"Okay, just let us know next time you're not feeling well so that we can get your coworkers to cover for you in time should the same thing happen. Okay?"

Oh my God, it worked.

"Yes, Linda, thank you for that." Skyler got up from the three-seater.

"All right, we'll see you on Monday, first thing in the morning," she chirped, like a bird.

"Okay. Bye."

Whew!

He turned the phone off with glee.

Skyler knew he was lying through his teeth. He had no intention of going back to work, what with the sorry shape he was in. He will just brush it off on Monday, as he did today. After all:

They need me more than I need them.

━━━

Skyler took the Depakote and Risperdal as directed, starting with the prescribed dosages of both medications, at ten o'clock in the evening of the same day he had the prescriptions filled. He glumly accepted medication compliance as an axe to grind. After all, didn't he want to get better? That thought seemed to take him down a slippery slope. Maybe he didn't want to get better. It was a case of the "fuck-its."

Fuck this. Fuck that. I don't give a flying fuck.

Skyler didn't really know if he wanted to get better. These mental gymnastics preoccupied him with the very first dose he took.

What an order! I can't go through with it.

These thoughts made him depressed. And with the depression, in trickled those same voices from inside his head, as if a demon were inside him — and then also from the outside, as if someone were speaking to him.

Why don't you overdose on your psych meds? At least they would be used for the right reasons.

Just then, the phone rang. And just as suddenly as the cacophony of voices terrified Skyler, then just as suddenly, with a whoosh of air, the raucous noises disappeared. Terrified but also relieved, Skyler answered the ring.

"Hello?" Skyler cradled his head in his hands.

"Skyler? Is that you?"

Oh, I know who this is. Thank God!

"Hi, Aunt Nancy. I'm here." Skyler exhaled.

"How do you feel?" He wondered if he should lie.

"Like shit."

Lying is a sin, to loved ones. But not to faceless corporations like Raleigh Studios.

"Aw, you'll feel better. Are you taking the medication like the doctor ordered?"

Don't fib, man!

"Just started. I don't feel better." Skyler looked down dejectedly.

"You have to give it a fair shake, don't you think? We love you, Skyler."

He looked back up and straightened his legs. "I

don't love myself." He said it matter-of-factly, as if it were obvious.

His aunt implored him. "Just follow the doctor's orders and go see Eleanor once a week, like she said."

"Okay, Aunt Nancy. I will."

"Okay, love you. Bye."

"Bye," he whispered audibly, as he held back tears.

Skyler wanted to believe that everyone around him was rooting for him, but he did not dare. That would mean that the overwhelmingly high dike that guarded him from the ocean of guilt and shame would collapse. Then he would have wrapped himself up in layers of self-protectiveness. He didn't let the truth happen to him, because his truth would buckle under the onslaught. It was time for a different approach. The current pain was just too great, and he unnecessarily held onto the hurt.

Skyler decided to play Pyotr Tchaikovsky's violin concerto in D major, Op. 35, performed by violinist Jascha Heifetz and Fritz Reiner conducting the Chicago Symphony Orchestra. Only Heifetz could play it the way it should be played — nothing but the complete exploitation of all the possibilities of the instrument. It was a big concerto, bigger than the Grieg piano concerto, bigger than Beethoven's Fifth

"Emperor" piano concerto. All-enveloping, all-encompassing, all-enrapturing. The melodies were haunting in the fast first and third sections, beautiful in the second, slow section. With music like this, life could go on despite all its trials and tribulations.

But toward the end, even the most life-affirming music could not reach Skyler at this hour. Miserable, he lay down on the leather three-seater, curled up in the fetal position, and held his head in his hands. He cried to himself quietly, with no one to talk to, until the medication took hold and overpowered him into sleep. Maybe he did need talk therapy and psych meds just as much, if not more so, than music. In just over a half hour, just as the very last note of the concerto was performed, it was "lights out" for Skyler.

⬭

OCTOBER - WEEK 2

Things were going nowhere, from bad to worse. Linda, his supervisor at Raleigh Studios, was getting increasingly flustered with Skyler. At lunchtime on Monday, she called him. He ignored her and once again decided to go AWOL.

The hell with her and all of those corporate fat cats.

Nevertheless, he had thoroughly enjoyed all the perks of being a corporate fat cat himself: season tickets to the Los Angeles Dodgers, a golf membership to the Wilshire Country Club, the corner office in the company C-suite. But his attitude stunk, and he kept trying to justify his behavior to himself.

I couldn't care less about holding down even a promising job. I've got ten K lying around. And I'll use all of it. And I don't care what happens next, after that.

Right now, once awake after a rough start and end to yesterday — his first day in West Hollywood, his last day in the Hollywood Hills, and no more days at work — he still felt rather unwell: headache, nausea, chills, irritable bowel syndrome, heartburn, even a throbbing toothache. But never mind those. He needed to focus on titrating up to the full dosage in two weeks, then assessing the situation with Dr. Wilson in four weeks.

━━━

Skyler worried that his telehealth sessions with Ms. Martinez would be combative, adversarial, and confrontational. More than anything else, they seemed to be a frustrating, plain old waste of time. On the following Monday after she and Skylar had an in-person in-take session at her Larchmont Village office, Martinez asked in their telehealth session, "So where should we begin?"

"Where do *you* think we should begin?" Skyler

snarled "I didn't ask for schizoaffective! You gave it to me."

"I gave you a tentative diagnosis. It's not who you are, it's what you have. It can be properly treated and medicated. So where would you like to begin?"

"I don't know. I suppose with my Uncle Frank. Before my dad died, I was given a trust fund that promised I would be taken care of. But Uncle Frank is now the executor in place of my dad, and he told me he can't give it to me since, according to him, I'm mentally incapacitated."

"But what exactly does it mean to you that you're mentally incapacitated, according to Uncle Frank?"

"It just means that I can't make common-sense decisions by myself. As if my judgment stinks. Like, what I would do with the money?"

"What would you do with the money if you had it?"

"I would spend a third, save a third, and give the final third away to charity. Like Carnegie or Rockefeller, you know? Because they had done a lot of bad, so they needed to do a lot of good too."

"Sounds sensible to me, although you might want to wait until you are further along in life and career before you became a philanthropist. Andrew

Carnegie and John Rockefeller were at the ends of their careers before doling out funds."

"Quit blowing the wind out of my sails!" Skyler yelled. Yet he knew Ms. Martinez was right. He just would not put his defenses down, even for a second. He was a porcupine, all prickly on the outside, all soft on the inside. He was both very unpleasantly on the defensive and also very unenjoyably on the offensive.

"Let's talk about your family, Skyler."

He exhaled and felt his palms start to sweat. "What about my family?"

"Why bother with your Uncle Frank? He is obviously no friend of yours, apparently. But he is the only connection to your deceased family that you have. He is your father's brother, after all. Can I suggest we talk about your sister?"

"Oh, why don't you suggest nothing at all!" Skyler yelled, before jabbing the "Leave" icon with the mouse on his laptop.

"Hold on, hold on —" Martinez tried to finish before getting disconnected.

Now Skyler was explosively irritable, whereas before this abbreviated session, he was quietly morose. With such mercurial moods, he easily changed from cold to hot.

OCTOBER - WEEK 3

By the end of the second week of taking medication, when he was required to increase the dosage, he noticed some rather peculiar and disturbing side effects.

The Risperdal for Skyler caused galactorrhea, or the production of breast tissue — and not just in women, but in men as well. To his horror, he was growing female teats. At first, he could not believe it, and he refused to believe it. He was not told it could happen, and he did not bother reading the fine print on the list of potential side effects provided with the bottle.

He grabbed at his pectoral muscles. They had become flabby, extending outward and downward.

Is this real?
That's just your imagination!
No, man, I'm telling you, it's true!
You just need to exercise those flabby muscles!

He grew increasingly terrified.

And the Depakote was no joke, either. In two weeks, he had gained fifteen pounds, from 165 lbs. to 180 lbs. Weight gain was a common side effect of Depakote, and the average was in fact fifteen pounds. But this was in a matter of two weeks only. Small solace, this fact did not make a now-pudgy Skyler feel good nor look good. His belly curved outward, giving the natural curvature of his spine an odd appearance. In the mirror he looked strange to himself, as if he were pregnant. The boyish good looks and homeless waif-like charm had vanished. He grabbed cheeky jowls where there had never been flab before.

What the hell is this?

He constantly went out for Pizza Hut and Domino's, Popeyes and Kentucky Fried Chicken, as well as McDonald's and Burger King, because the feeling of being satisfyingly full (satiation) now required much more food to achieve than he previously needed. That was the physical aspect of the Depakote's side effect — weight gain.

I should go on a diet and do more exercise, I guess...

But the problem was also psychological. Metaphorically, Skyler was trying to fill a void in his stomach that could not be filled, like a black hole that sucked everything into it that came its way. That black hole, whether a hidden trauma or an unearthed conflict, could make itself felt by impeding psychological progress that would otherwise unplug blockage in the stomach. Instead, the blockage got worse and worse as more and more food made Skyler's system balloon out of proportion.

Maybe I need to overcome my own resistance to getting better.

All this time to himself, and it did not even occur to him that his job was in jeopardy. Except for one thing: he recognized his supervisor calling him (again), two weeks after he had promised to return.

He had been AWOL for two whole weeks, not calling in his return, not calling in sick.

I bet my whole work team has been scrambling to fill the void. Damn, I'm managing a whole team of creative people at corporate. And I thought I had hidden all my problems from everybody at work. Not to mention we were all ready to make that deal with Paramount Studios go through.
They really needed me!
Whew, I screwed everybody over there, even the CEO, and Jesus, now I'm screwed...

Skyler hit himself over the head with a closed fist. Disgusted with his fat, lazy self, but knowing that this was all his own doing, he did not answer her call. Now there was a voicemail afterward. He dialed his phone, and the inevitable came to pass, as he winced with pain and anticipated the worst news:

"Hi, Skyler, it's Linda Pfeffer. We'll have to let you go, in no uncertain terms. Don't worry too much. Please do not contact us, in any manner, because you let the entire organization down when we could have used you the most during this Paramount deal. Now Raleigh Studios is in deep trouble. I'll have your office stuff boxed up and ready for you to pick up anytime next week. Best wishes on your future career, Skyler." *Click.*

Of course, there was no guarantee he was going to make the effort to pick up his stuff from work, either!

After two more weeks, when he was scheduled to meet with Dr. Wilson — and with a protruding belly and protruding nipples — Skyler turned on the telehealth connection on his laptop.

"Hi, Skyler! How are you?" All bubbly.

"Why'd you do this to me?" Anger filled the void between doctor and patient.

"I'm sorry." Dr. Wilson's easygoing manner stiffened, "Skyler, what did I do to you?"

"You never mentioned any side effects of these meds! Look at me!" He took off his shirt. "Look at this. I have tits and I'm twenty-five pounds heavier."

"I'm so sorry, Skyler. We can put you on different meds, if you like. We can always try something different until we get to the right cocktail that works for you."

"Oh, and so I'm a guinea pig?" Skyler began to weep in despair.

"I didn't mean that. Let's titrate you off the Risperdal and Depakote. I think I know what will work for you, and without the side effects." The doctor maintained an aura of professionalism.

"Then why did you put me on this stuff in the first place? I quit! I fucking quit!"

"Now hold on, Skyler. Most of the time, these medications do work. It's just not the case with you. Not all hope is lost."

"I want something that erases my emotions and makes me forget about my family." Skyler's tone of voice broke, and he conveyed his true wish.

"There is no medication that will erase your emotions and make you forget about your family. It would be best for you to reestablish your therapy with Ms. Martinez. Work through your emotions with her by talking about your family."

"Then why am I talking to you? Who is in charge here?"

"Please understand that I will get you on some better medications."

"To hell with your meds! You have pissed me off for the last time. Fuck you!"

"C'mon, Skyler, let me..." *Doink!* Skyler ended the meeting unilaterally.

Feeling sky-high irritable before the conversation

but feeling down-in-the-doldrums depressed after, Skyler made up his mind. He was free of any obligation to his now-defunct treatment team. He no longer looked back to his previous support system — family and physicians — but looked forward to taking his chances and sailing the unknown, untested waters of Los Angeles.

OCTOBER - WEEK 4

Skyler needed some drugs — some "real" drugs, something that would take away the physical pain and make him forget his mental distress. He pulled out from his phone an e-contact he never thought he would have to call: Reggie, his party buddy from college, the one who had aided his drug-fueled outburst at Uncle Frank's earlier on, possibly because Reggie swapped cocaine for PCP. Or so Skyler suspected.

"Yo, man. Hit me up if you want to party," he had said to Skyler during the cap-and-gown cere-mony. "I'm moving into Hollywood, and I got a super nice dig, set up far away from all the dumb shit in Westwood." Skyler never thought he would go to a lowlife illicit drug dealer for help, but desperate times called for desperate measures.

Skyler called Reggie.

The drug dealer answered, "Yo, who's this?"

"Reggie? It's Skyler from UCLA. Do you remember me?"

"Skyler, Skyler. Oh, yeah, bro. How you be?"

"Fine, man. You know, I was wondering if we could get together sometime."

Skyler drove from West Hollywood, leaving his possessions behind in his apartment, to the heart of "Hollyweird." The address, 1776 N. Sycamore Avenue, was close to the intersection of Hollywood Boulevard and La Brea Avenue. Skyler parked his car on the side of the road, making sure to raise his ragtop and lock the doors electronically. He did not think that he would need a security system on the BMW 325i, but he still took all the necessary precautions. He did not want his car to be stolen. There were a lot of crooks in this town.

Up the front stairs and then buzzing on the intercom.

"Yo, who's this?" There was unveiled suspicion in his voice.

"Hey, Reggie, it's Sky." He dropped the end to his name to sound cool.

"All right, I'll let you in, dog." The voice registered acceptance.

Once indoors, he made his way to Unit 307. There was a faint odor of marijuana, although it was suffused in the air, hence hard to pinpoint. A simple knock, and the door opened a crack, with Reggie's head sticking out.

Looking up and down the hallway, Reggie exclaimed, much to Skyler's relief, "Hey, man, we're just in the middle of a session. Haha, come on in!"

Reggie was a curious-looking character. His corpulent body was partially hidden underneath baggy jeans and oversized T-shirts, but they didn't quite do the job of completely covering his heavy belly and "man-tits," just as Skyler now had himself. Reggie's face was evilly ugly, even misshapen, with a set of conniving, beady eyes that told you that all manner of disreputable and shady dealings were being cooked up in his mind. Skyler did not trust this modern-day Shakespearean Falstaff, whom he thought was either a psychopath or, in close second, a sociopath. He was, after all, a drug dealer whose livelihood involved destroying other people's lives. Not to mention two people in his apartment who caught Skyler's attention.

Reggie introduced his guests: "Skyler, this is Jeanne, my girlfriend."

Or so he says. I bet she doesn't put out at all, haha.

She extended a hand, which Skyler clasped (*Ee-ooh, clammy!*) while she offered a cold, slit-eyed stare. "And this is Josie, her friend." Josie offered her hand, which Skyler instinctively took.

Oh, so warm and dry!

He bent over and kissed her hand as he felt the old chivalry.

Dude, you just met this girl. You're crazy, man, you're crazy.

She registered a wholesome, modest smile.

Skyler wondered why a good-looking girl like Jeanne was with such an ugly guy like Reggie. Was she tired of going out with good-looking guys who treated her like crap, so therefore Reggie was a gentleman? Actually, it was more a matter of low self-esteem. But he found out later that that answer was in Josie's purview. She was Jeanne's best friend, who ensured that Jeanne didn't fall for this guy who had a reputation in college for deflowering underage high school girls. Jeanne was perched uneasily between Josie and Reggie, and Reggie was winning the tug-of-war.

Maybe I need to throw my weight in here somewhere.

He found Jeanne's beauty to be very shallow, one that wore out and generated nausea over time. To Skyler, such beauty attracted dirt, precisely because it was trashiness and garbage itself. There were no pretensions here to high classiness nor well-deserved snobbery.

Skyler found Josie to be much better-looking than Jeanne. Josie was not as racy nor as fast-looking as to be chased by all types of boys as Jeanne was. Some guys might even call Josie a bit dumpy, even a bit dingy. But she exuded a genuine, honest-to-goodness innocence and wholesomeness that were very appealing to Skyler. Such appeal grew over time for him, and that was a big part of her attractiveness to him.

Like a bottle of wine, I guess?

No, this was no bottle of wine! This was a young lady whose class and distinction lent her personal charm. He wanted to know so much more about this blushing maiden, for him to gain the glory for defending her honor and life.

The acrid, heavy smell of pot shot straight up through Skyler's nostrils.

Contact high. So, the smell in the hallway did emanate from here!

Reggie began his psychological interrogation, "What's been going on with you since UCLA?"

"Oh, nothing much. Lost my family a couple years ago to a car crash. My uncle is trying to control my finances. They say I have a mental health diagnosis, but I don't want therapy and medication. I don't think there's anything wrong with me."

Jeanne's eyeballs swung to the right at Reggie, then all the way to the left at Josie. Both made eye contact with Jeanne. However, Reggie seemed to express pathetic disgust. But to Josie? Warm compassion.

"Of course, there ain't nothing wrong with you, man," Reggie stated matter-of-factly, sensing a weakness, a vulnerability, with that beady-eyed smile of his that did not look at you but into you and through you. "It's all in your head. Here, man, take a hit. This will make all your problems go away."

Reggie offered a water bong with the bowl packed with pot. Skyler had seen this one before. It was a squat sort of thing made of red plastic. You sucked up the smoke through a chamber containing water, which cooled the smoke. They called it the "Red Monster" on campus from back in the day. And now here it was, returned to him.

"Okay, man, let me hit that," Skyler said. Reggie lit the fully packed bowl. Skyler sucked in, smoke collected, then Reggie lifted his thumb from a hole in the tube to create a suction, and the smoke swooshed into Skyler's unsuspecting mouth. *Whoa!* Skyler sputtered in a series of coughs as the girls laughed — with him, or at him? At this point it was not really clear. Maybe Jeanne laughed at him, while Josie laughed with him.

"Whoa, that hit the spot!" Skyler shook his head.

The sensation emerged. Instantly, he was swept back to his college days, when he felt the release from responsibility and accountability with just one bong hit. The beautiful light-headedness, the wonderful floating in the cloudy ether, the untrammeled gleeful playfulness, the music sounding unbelievably that much better. Everything gone — pain gone, suffering gone, memories gone — even life itself, gone, gone, gone. It was an escape from everything that the pothead sought, even if it were only temporary. Eventually returning to reality was fine only so long as there was enough marijuana to catapult the user back to the high.

Skyler hung out a little longer to sober up from the pot, and also to buy a quarter-ounce of the same stuff, before he politely declined more pot from a grandiose Reggie, who apparently wanted to make a great impression on the females. Skyler said his good-byes to Jeanne in a rudely polite manner and to Josie in a politely respectful tone, then he headed for the door. He hugged Reggie good-naturedly and stated emphatically, "Hey, Reggie. We gotta hang out more often."

"You got it, dog!"

Finally, Skyler drove back to West Hollywood to decompress from all the socializing. But he did not gradually taper off the Depakote and Risperdal properly. He had also mixed the residual medication in his system with THC, the active ingredient in marijuana. Once he was inside his apartment, he collapsed onto the leather three-seater and passed out.

But then he was haunted by the memory of the car crash that happened to his family. The voices reemerged even stronger than before, and the sickening drive to mania made him jump right out of his skin.

Was it just a bad dream? Or a terrifying nightmare?

Wait! It was just a nightmare!

He had woken up in the middle of the night, shortly after passing out, shivering in the cold October air, buck naked, running around the building courtyard as if he were in the Los Angeles marathon and could not get enough of the smoggy air. No one was around when he did the sprint finish, but the building's surveillance cameras were, and they caught everything for Olga. He woke up, yet again, this time wildly conscious, his bad-smelling clothes in a pile on the floor, his unbrushed bad breath emanating from his mouth, his bad body odor reeking from his armpits, everything. He heard something going to voicemail, and eager to pick up to

Reggie, Jeanne or Josie, he answered it. But it was that female's Eastern European accent coming through the speaker.

"Mr. Jones, this is your apartment manager Olga informing you that you have been evicted from your apartment due to excessive noise which has been coming from your space. And also, your running naked down the hallways and around the courtyard did not help things either. We will need you to be out of there by Monday at the latest, and please don't make any more noise until then. Have a nice day." *Click.*

Oh, no!

Skyler should have known that it was a flash back to the past: incomprehensible screaming, bashing chords on his electronic keyboard, mixing loud CDs of electronic dance music, taking off his clothes, running around naked in the yard. Well...at least he didn't spray-paint graffiti on the walls (they were unmarked, upon inspection).

Okay, I guess I fucked that one up.

Skyler put on yesterday's outfit, lugged his voluminous wardrobe into the backseat of his car, carefully detached his keyboard from the collapsible stand as well as from the power cord before depositing it into the trunk, carefully placed his CD catalog and CD mixer into the floor of the backseats, and finally, put his laptop on the passenger seat, right where he could see and access it. Perched on his head was Emily's raver lid, making him feel young, sexy, and cool.

━━

After a few extended moments wallowing in misery, Skyler got his bearings. He detached the apartment keys and garage door opener from his BMW keyholder and marched over to the leasing office.

Once there, he spied Olga at her desk. When he opened the door, she looked up from some paperwork and greeted him with a barely contained scowl.

"I'm sorry, Olga. I don't know what else to say." He handed over the items.

This time, her scowl softened a bit. She asked him, "Where are you going to go now?" in that thick Eastern European accent of hers.

"I don't know. Wherever the day takes me, I guess..." An air of abject detachment overcame him.

Olga nodded off a bit. "Okay. Good luck," she said, sensing something a lot bigger on his hands than just a broken lease. But she herself could not be bothered.

He walked out with a sad smile. Afterward, he sat listlessly in the driver's seat for a full minute, unsure of where to go next. Then he decided and backed out to skid away.

As dusk approached, Skyler chose to use the space available to him in his car. Ultimately, it was just a possession, like any other. For the first time in his life, he made do with makeshift linens — his wardrobe — thrown about in the backseat, where he would lie down. And he simply parked for the night on a side street, away from the streetlights, to cut down on noise and light pollution.

Living on the street soon became all-too-familiar to him.

Necessity is the mother of invention.

He laughed inappropriately at his own joke. Thank God nobody was around to hear Skyler cackle.

He lay down among his clothes, and it seemed that it was not too far-fetched to use a car like a bed, sort of like how RVs are, except smaller in scale. He looked up at the ragtop, which was somewhat claustrophobically close.

Ah, it's okay!

Then he tried to lock his knees and straighten out. But couldn't do it. The car was not wide enough to handle his height. He bent his knees, threw one leg over the passenger seat, and tried to lie diagonally to make maximum use of the space. It hurt his back.

Goddamn...

Then he used a genius tactic — crawl up in the fetal position, hold your head in your hands, and do not pay attention to anything or anybody that comes near the car. He slept fitfully. He woke up a few times in the middle of the night because of the Los Angeles winter nighttime cold. But the raver's lid kept his head warm.

The next day, sleeping in a car became quite tiresome to him. Skyler did a U-turn in the narrow side street and parked his BMW in a motel parking lot off Sunset Boulevard somewhere in Hollywood. What a seedy place! Sickeningly orange paint peeled off the doors and windows. Rusty staircases and untreated pool water showed the sad state of repair. Making sure that no one was scoping out the territory for his luxury vehicle, Skyler parked away from the main drag, far into the small lot.

From the Chinese motel manager on call who spoke in singsong English, Skyler bought a room for a hundred bucks a night. It was what he needed for the time being, although the daily rate would certainly add up over time. Plus, he was unemployed, so he needed to husband his resources as he pondered his next move. For now, he reveled in the cleansing shower, changing leisurely into clean clothes (albeit a gray pinstripe suit), and sleeping relatively comfortably under clean sheets. Of course, other than these creature comforts, there was not much else that the motel offered. Just an ancient television set with basic cable and a tattered *TV Guide* set on top of it.

No room service here!

Skyler would have to order Chinese delivery to compete with the McDonald's down the street.

For a few days, he lived out of the motel room, but he didn't like how it was up one flight of stairs while his car and all his possessions were down in the parking lot. But he did not want to be seen lugging his valuable stuff up the stairs and into the room, in broad daylight. Maybe he could have done it at night? But then all that fluorescent lighting would have caught him in the act, and he didn't want to run into anybody who was living out of their own motel rooms seeing him carrying his life possessions into his.

The keyboard had cost nearly ten grand because the keys were made of wood, not plastic, and the keyboard action mimicked that of a true grand piano action, better than any other electronic keyboard on the market at that time. The CDs were irreplaceable, since they had been culled from thousands upon thousands of hours spent listening to music to cultivate and refine Skyler's taste. And the CD mixer was top of the line. It had the most advanced audio technology and all the "bells and whistles" electronics to give a DJ the widest latitude in making music. The device featured every advantage, which had set Skyler back thousands of dollars. And he had had those couple-dozen snazzy suits all custom-tailored for him, when he had the money for it. Those were priceless, but chances were that they would fit him poorly now, what with all his ballooning weight. Normally, he was a 42 Regular in the chest with a

36-inch waist, meaning a standard, proportional 6-inch drop. But now he would need a 44 Short and a 38-inch waist. His current suits would fit him very tightly, very uncomfortably, and he would not look good either.

Of course, there was a third possibility, but Skyler liked it least. Perhaps he could grovel to Reggie, that lecherous bastard, to see if he could crash on his couch in the living room. He would use the excuse that he was too much under the influence to drive anywhere, even short distances.

⬒

"Say, Reggie?" Skyler prompted himself with a pathetic plaintiveness. It was ten o'clock on a Sunday evening. The female guests had gone home, acknowledging that tomorrow was a workday, and the party would have to end early.

"Yeah, what?" Reggie was on Cloud Nine, reclining on the couch. His eyes were closed dreamily, and his mouth was hanging open. Drool started to collect and dribble down.

"Can I stay here tonight?"

Oh, no.

The smarmy tone in Skyler's voice was a complete buzz kill. Reggie's eyes opened just a little, and his mouth closed. He looked at Skyler out of the corners of his eyes. He was suddenly off Cloud Nine and back to reality. "You wanna do *what?*" Suspicion permeated the air.

"Stay here, you know? I'm too fucked up to drive anywhere right now. I need to sleep my high off." Skyler shrugged his shoulders, as if doing so would make his request more sensible. Silence fell upon Reggie as he considered Skyler's request, and an ugly frown materialized on his face. All Skyler could do was teeter from one leg to the other nervously. Finally, after cold calculation, and after considering the costs and the benefits, Reggie decided on the following.

"All right, man. But only one night, Sky. I don't want you hanging around here acting as if you own the place. Besides, you owe me for that extra eighth of weed you smoked. C'mon, man, I need payback."

And so, Reggie put Skyler on the defensive and made him feel small enough to motivate him to be out of there by sunrise, one minute after which Reggie threatened to forcefully kick him in the face for his tardiness. However, Skyler, who was stuck there out of necessity because of a raging hangover, slept in until 10 o'clock the next morning, which infuriated Reggie, who tried to find any advantage he could out of Skyler's indiscretion.

"C'mon, you bum. This ain't your place. Get the hell up, man! Don't you remember all the weed you smoked? Pony up, punk!"

Thus, Skyler, in a pot-induced stupor, completely out of sorts, and looking quite like the stereotypical homeless person lying all passed-out on a park bench, had to search frantically through his pockets for thirty bucks in cash to appease Reggie.

There is no free lunch.

NOVEMBER
ABANDON ALL HOPE

NOVEMBER - WEEK 1

At the beginning of November, Skyler was completely estranged from Uncle Frank and Aunt Nancy. He wanted to plead his case one last time, to seek some sort of financial reconciliation. But he was also afraid, not of them, but of himself.

I still have a soft spot for them in my heart. I feel I should not go to their house in the Hollywood Hills. I'm worried that I might get physical with them. That's a line I refuse to cross, even though I have so much rage inside me I want to punch the living daylights out of Uncle Frank and chase Aunt Nancy back into her house!

So, instead of going to their house, he called

them one fateful day at ten in the morning. He sat in his BMW, elbows resting on the steering wheel, one hand holding onto the phone, the other hand holding onto his head.

Uncle Frank picked up. "Hello, Skyler?"

"Yeah, Uncle Frank, it's me. I'm asking you, please, give me some of the trust fund money that you're managing for me." His arms rocked back and forth.

"Skyler, for the zillionth time, I can't do that." Uncle Frank rolled his eyes.

Doesn't this kid get it?

"Why can't you? That's my money. You have no right to withhold it from me like this!" One elbow slipped and sounded the horn accidentally.

"Skyler, you're not making a bit of sense. You can work. Everyone else does. So why can't you?" Uncle Frank raised his voice up a notch.

"Uncle Frank, I'm too fucked up to work. Dr. Wilson's medications didn't work and had massive side effects. And Ms. Martinez's pointless psychobabble only focused on my past family history. And finally, you're not stepping up to the plate. I'm falling through the cracks, Uncle Frank, I'm falling through the cracks!" Skyler's tone of voice grated under the stress.

"Skyler, you haven't given the treatment team we set up for you a fair try. You think that in two months' time —" Uncle Frank tried to make his point.

"One month, dammit, it's been *one* month." Skyler pumped the brake pedal over and over with his foot.

"Okay, Okay, one month. But don't you see what I mean? You didn't give it a snowball's chance in hell. Look at Emily's case, how long it took — " Frank felt as if he were talking to a petulant child.

"Don't talk about Emily, Uncle Frank. You don't know her the way I did." Tears welled up in Skyler's eyes. And that was when the voice came after him.

Drive yourself over a cliff. At least we can salvage the car.

Sky dropped the phone in his lap and put his head in both hands in abject futility. On the other end of the line, Uncle Frank simply shook his head in a display of utter hopelessness.

As Skyler picked his phone back up, his uncle concluded, "Skyler, you are perfectly capable of working. You're just not trying to find a job which is fulfilling for you. Look, you have to do the therapy and give enough time for the meds to kick in. Once you're stable, I will gladly hand over the money that does in fact belong to you. But not before. And, sorry to say this, but I have a sinking feeling that given your weakened state, you would frivolously spend any financial resources from the trust fund that I gave you. You get it?"

Skyler countered with, "Okay, Uncle Frank. But if you were honest and truthful, you'd see that the trust fund money would go a long way to making my life more stable. Going after gainful employment all the time deforms my emotional growth and development. If you were truly compassionate, you would give some money to me for now, until I show that I am ready for more."

Seeing that neither side would change the other's views. and seeing the pointlessness of raising his voice to nearly incomprehensible screaming, Skyler shut his phone off. He was too riled up by the exchange of emotional gunfire. So, he decided to smoke some pot to stop "the voice" from getting too out of hand. He was scared by its random nature. It would get louder and louder and louder before retreating unexpectedly to the background. Its arbitrary nature was most frightening. He just wished it would go away, forever!

———

By November, Skyler was a regular customer and partygoer at Reggie's pad, and he had graduated from pot to powder. The only redeeming quality for him in Reggie's eyes was his savings account. One time, it was the four of them: Reggie and Jeanne on the "A-list" of cool trendsetters, with Skyler and Josie on the "B-list" of uncool hangers-on. Eric Clapton's tune "Cocaine" drifted throughout Reggie's pad and lent a warm, romantic touch to what was otherwise a cold, sterile procedure.

Reggie took a plastic bag full of white stuff that mostly had the consistency of baby powder but also had some small crystals in it. He gently poured about a tablespoon of it onto his coffee table, where the glass panels made for a smooth surface. To the small pile, he took a razor blade and expertly cut down the crystals in the powder so that the stuff more or less had the same fine consistency. Up and down, side to side, chop chop chop. It seemed mesmerizingly effortless.

Then Reggie queried his wingman, "Yo, Sky. Why don't you take a hit?"

"What is it?" Skyler leaned forward.

"Cocaine. Blow. Yeyo."

"Okay!"

"Here, man." Reggie offered him a tightly rolled-up dollar bill. Instinctively, Skyler put one end of the dollar bill up one nostril with one hand and closed the other nostril with the index finger of the other hand. He bent over the glass top of the coffee table and closed his mouth to make sure not to scatter the line nor disturb the pile of cocaine. He positioned the other end of the dollar bill at the beginning of the line. He snorted in quickly through his nose while moving up the line to move the stuff through the makeshift tube and up Skyler's nostril.

Expert marksmanship!

Thirty seconds later, Skyler felt it. A "no-nonsense" cocaine buzz was what it was, not at all a sloppy alcoholic buzz, nor in the least a cloudy marijuana buzz. It made sense that high-powered corporate types did cocaine exclusively. It was not just expensive, but it also helped you put all your affairs in order. You could actually work more productively and efficiently with this narcotic.

But in a social setting, there was another byproduct of the buzz. It made Skyler talk as if he were the most knowledgeable chatterbox in all of Hollywood. "Did you know that Hollywood was founded in 1887?" He had an opinion on everything, and he would also explain those opinions at length: "I think the Middle East problem would be best resolved if..." A sense of triumphant euphoria, energy, and mental alertness cut through Skyler's brain fog and produced razor-sharp clarity. He was no longer tormented by the voice, and he stopped losing touch with reality.

Ecstasy was a similar yet different experience. A euphoric and energizing high lifted the mental fog, similar to cocaine. And it generated mental alertness. But ecstasy felt warmer, more empathic, more "touchy-feely." It lacked the razor-shop edge that gave cocaine-users an advantage. Rather, ecstasy users gained "collegial" feelings, as if the experience were strictly a noncompetitive exercise.

Skyler noticed how ecstasy brought Reggie and Jeanne together:

"Hey, babe. How ya feelin'?" Reggie playfully tapped Jeanne's leg.

"Oh, I'm doin' just fine." Jeanne massaged Reggie's shoulder.

"You know I have feelings for you, right?" Reggie gave her a grotesque smile (according to Skyler, that is).

Jeanne jovially acknowledged Reggie's advances, "I know that, sweetie."

Of course, a non-drug user would notice how artificial and contrived such feelings were. Perhaps ecstasy was the only way that Jeanne and Reggie could truly bond with each other, let alone with others. They apparently could not do otherwise without it. Of course, nothing took away from the drug its near-miracle "Make love, not war" property. But Skyler concluded, right from the very beginning, that he was not supposed to feel this good about himself.

In the drug dealer's lair, there were yet other powders to choose from. Each powder represented a different buzz, one that could be identified by its "flavor" or "taste." Skyler thought half-jokingly to himself that the buzz of cocaine made you chatty, the euphoria of ecstasy left you blissful, the edge of crystal methamphetamine propped your attitude up, and the roar of ketamine vanquished your depression. These drugs were amazingly intense and just as amazingly effective at getting Skyler out of his funk, voice-free (one would add). He became the perfect guest — courteous, polite, charismatic, and charming. Everybody liked him. He even liked himself!

During November, all ten-thousand dollars of Skyler's savings were fully engaged in purchasing drugs. Reggie coached him on how to spend the money — which was still going to line the dealer's own pockets. But Skyler wanted to bankroll the party, even if as a spoiled rich kid whose overwhelming feelings of guilt and grief were still consuming him from the inside out. However, the two ladies in the rest of the group welcomed him. Of course, Jeanne had a more nefarious reason for approving Skyler's stay — the money. And of course, Josie had a more benevolent reason for approving his stay — the community.

With $2,500 each week committed for four weeks, each week consisted of four days — Friday through Monday — of partying with three days' rest and relaxation — Tuesday through Thursday — from the debauchery. Therefore, $400 daily for drugs, which were divvied up for the four powders for him and his party "friends" Jeanne and Reggie: a) cocaine, b) ecstasy, c) crystal methamphetamine, and d) ketamine. An additional $100 daily allotment went to pot for everybody, especially for Josie, since she didn't do the powders (it was a consolation prize). And for the R&R days of Tuesday through Thursday, Skyler would spend the remaining $500 (not much) on living expenses. He was becoming quite the bon vivant in all this. As long as he could supply the money to front the cost, then he was a happy druggie, Reggie was a successful "businessman," Jeanne dangerously courted disgrace, Josie increasingly suffered anxiety, and the endless partying careened full speed ahead into oblivion.

━━

NOVEMBER - WEEK 2

As it were, cocaine and ecstasy were more Skyler's "speed." The edge of crystal meth was too "sharp" for his senses, while the roar of ketamine came across as too tranquilizing. As November progressed, the short-term effects of cocaine and ecstasy wore off quickly, and the long-term effects of their usage became apparent. Each caused a noticeable side effect — weight loss as a result of diminishing appetite. Instead of chasing after food, the addict chased after the next high. But put together, cocaine and ecstasy would make an addict totally waste away. True, Skyler needed this weight loss as a counter to the weight gain caused by the Depakote. But going up, and then coming down, and then overshooting the mark, wreaked havoc on the addict's physiology.

If someone asked Skyler, "Why those two?" he would probably have said, "I don't really know. I guess I just like the highs." Just as Skyler did not know previously what the Depakote and Risperdal were supposed to do to his brain, he also did not know exactly what the powders were doing to his brain. This lack of understanding certainly made their abuse that much more abominable in the eyes of the non-user than it appeared to the user.

But his behavior spoke to the confusion. After many more lines of coke, Skyler became "Mr. Sky-high," yelling semi-intelligibly, "You're not real! You're not real! You're not real! I'm the boss! I'm the boss! I'm the boss!" to Reggie while giggling menacingly and not realizing in the moment that *you don't bite the hand that feeds you,* especially in front of others. Skyler embarrassed Reggie and made him look like a party host who could not manage his guests.

Jeanne gave Skyler a nasty stare whenever he tried pointlessly to confront Reggie, through those slits for eyes, while she pulled on a cigarette. She whispered something in Reggie's ear, to which he nodded in agreement and then shook his head in disgust. And then she said out loud to Skyler: *"You're a fucking clown, man!"* And as the master of ceremonies, Reggie unceremoniously pushed Skyler away from the coffee table's glass top.

"Yo, man, I'm gonna lay down the law: no more lines for you tonight!" Reggie decided to put an end to the charade.

"Ah, c'mon, man, give me another hit," Skyler begged with hands together.

"No way, Jose. You're right on the line, Sky-high!" Polite but firm, as if he were looking out for Skyler's own good. In fact, Reggie was just out to shut him down. It was a subtle, strategic, and lopsided power struggle between the two. Skyler bankrolled the stream of powders. But Reggie knew how to supply them. If there were a disagreement, there was no contract that could be resorted to, unfortunately for Skyler. He wasn't ruthless, as Reggie was.

"Hey, Reggie, didn't I buy those lines for you?" Skyler questioned, trying to point out his own truth to the dealer.

"Well, if you want your money back, yo f'shaw can. But if you ask me, don't even try, don't even think about it, Mr. Sky-high." Reggie upped the ante.

And so, Reggie had Skyler right where he

wanted him, pining for another hit. He gave himself and Jeanne the supply of powders for the evening. Unless, of course, Skyler crawled on his belly, groveled to him, and said, "Hey, yo, Reggie, I'm really sorry I said that. I don't know what's wrong with me."

Reggie would then voice his suspicion, "Yo, man, what is wrong with you? Are you, like, crazy or something?" with a scowl and in a nasty tone of voice. And that was very alarming to Skyler. Somehow, his behavior was arousing the suspicion of those around him that he might be mentally ill. In the beginning of their relationship, he had mentioned to the group that he was considered mentally ill, but he had said he did not believe it. Now, starting with Reggie, perhaps he was mentally ill, and they *did* believe it.

I can't let them know about my mental health challenges.

"Yo, man, of course n-not!" Skyler managed to trip over his own well-rehearsed reply to Reggie's query.

"Because you can't hold your shit together for longer than fifteen minutes? Get it together or get lost," Reggie barked at Skyler. Reggie knew that such an ultimatum would win him favors from the ladies in the group. Skyler was starting to unravel externally in front of Jeanne and Josie, and they would probably side with Reggie to kick him out. But in a similar vein, if Skyler was worth more than his ten thousand, they might have struck gold, so Reggie knew keeping this trust-fund baby around would be a good thing.

Then, in a show of affected grandiosity, Reggie donated a couple of lines back to Skyler: "Here Sky-high, you get a little bit more," pushing some small, short lines to him but only after Jeanne and Reggie were finished with the lines that were still crystalline, pristine and powerful. "Jeanne and I get the good stuff, man, because we know how to party!" The two raised hands and gave each other high-fives.

Demoted in rank and dejected in spirit, Skyler sat down next to the other "party-pooper" and "buzz-killer," Josie. Reggie nicknamed her "Miz Dirt-down," as opposed to "Mr. Sky-high." She sat on the end of the couch, mostly out of range of Reggie's verbal jabs, which made her look away, shyly. Then, embarrassed, she would say, "I like pot, Reggie. Okay? Do you have a problem with that?" Skyler respected her because she refused to give in to peer pressure.

"Ah, no," Reggie replied. "But again, come on, Josie, everyone's doing it," Reggie sneered at her. Meanwhile, Jeanne ignored Josie's rather uncool rebuffing of his offers, except when they were about to leave. That was when Josie suddenly seemed so cool to Jeanne because, after all, she had to bum rides from Josie.

So, that's why Josie is important to the fractious functioning of the group! Jeanne needs a designated driver.

Meanwhile, to Skyler, his poor nose and that glass-top coffee table were the only things at issue. The distance between them was the only distance that mattered and that needed to be closed. That was all he could think of. Nothing else mattered.

⬚

While he was direct and forceful with Reggie about what he needed to party, Skyler was intentionally circumspect with the ladies. He always greeted Jeanne with "Hello, Ms. Lipton," and always approached Josie with "How are you, Ms. Heller?" He furtively watched Jeanne out of the corner of his eye to see whether she took Reggie's side or took Josie's side in the case of a split. For example, Reggie openly asked Jeanne to take another line when Josie signaled that it was time to go home. And what did Jeanne do? She excused herself momentarily — and conveniently — to the bathroom.

Skyler himself felt pulled in opposite directions. Reggie provided the powders as entertainment, but Skyler felt the need to support Josie's independence. He sat there on the couch, staying neutral, not taking sides, even though in his heart of hearts he knew with a sinking feeling that Reggie was the fire-spiting dragon and Josie was the damsel in distress. And Skyler knew, in his weakened emotional state, that he could not come to her protection nor defense.

One time, Skyler said, "I'm out," and got up to leave.

Josie quickly gathered her belongings and said, "Me, too!"

And that was when Jeanne (who normally did not leave without Josie) said, "All right, later, you two!" and that was exactly what Josie was worried about.

They walked down the hall and took the elevator to the first floor in silence. Outside on the curb, out of sight and sound to Reggie and Jeanne, Josie spoke first: "I'm losing Jeanne to that drug dealer. I guess they're sleeping with each other by now." She started to weep. This was the first time for Skyler that anybody in their group of four had said anything about rents in the social fabric.

"Hey, now. Come here!" Skyler offered outstretched arms and a wide-armed hug.

"Thanks, Sky. You seem to be a really nice guy who just wants to party, honey."

That tugged at Skyler's heartstrings and nearly melted his heart, right then and there.

Oh, dear. I'm gonna cry, too.

He had not expected such emotional warmth from somebody whom *he* thought was just a party-pooper.

Josie muffled her tears.

"You think that's who I am?" Skyler chuckled and let Josie out of his hug a good half-minute later. He dared not take sides too decisively in the power struggle with Reggie and Jeanne, on one hand, and with him and Josie, on the other hand, as it was turning out. Right now, Reggie and Jeanne had the upper hand, and it seemed unlikely that Skyler and Josie would win.

"Can I walk you to your car?" Skyler offered with an abundance of charm.

"Sure," accepted Josie, walking next to Skyler, stride by stride.

Once they got to her car, she gave Skyler a big bear-hug and lifted him off the sidewalk.

"Ah, put me down, put me down!" exclaimed Skyler, giggling like a little schoolgirl.

I like how she is. I'm starting to really dig her!

As she got in her car and drove away, he waved goodbye to her.

I have to be in her corner, somehow. I have to go to bat for her. How?

But Skyler's own chances of abandoning the sinking ship in time seemed remote at best. He was an addict. He was hooked. He was in deep trouble. He had gone down the path of no return. Could he still pull out in time? Instead of navigating a glide path, he was stuck in a nosedive. It would take every ounce of energy for him to avoid a crash and generate a safe landing.

How do I get myself away from Reggie's powder keg, and how do I get Josie into my sphere of influence?

▭

NOVEMBER - WEEK 3

As his finances dwindled and skidded toward near-nothing — just as his body wasted away and headed toward being rail-thin — Skyler pretty much went down and out in Hollywood and, moreover, began to engage in criminal acts of petty theft. One time in a sushi restaurant, he waited for his takeout order, which he could barely afford. Much to his surprise, he spied the glass tip jar open-mouthed with bills resting in it. It was on a table, away from the motorized carousel where the sushi moved, around and around. And some of the patrons had their backs to Skyler. The tip jar looked like an easy target. Thinking he was sly, he plucked a note — $20! — and stuck it into the inner side pocket of his cargo shorts. Upon getting his order, he made his way to the exit until he heard yelling behind him, then he saw the chef's assistant in front of him.

"Hold on a second, man," the guy barked at Skyler while blocking the exit.

Skyler feigned innocence. "What? What did I do?"

"We saw you take the tip," said another employee, coming close.

The yelling got louder and closer.

"Then check my pockets. I didn't take anything!"

A small crowd had gathered around Skyler, and the festive atmosphere in the restaurant ended with some curious customers trying to figure out what was going on.

The chef motioned to them, "Check his pockets."

They patted him down, the criminal that he was, and came up with nothing. Skyler's lucky out was the hidden pocket in his shorts. Their search unsuccessful, the employees bitterly went back to work. Skyler raised his arms at the chef, as if to say, "What happened?"

Then he walked out after paying for the meal with a nearly maxed-out credit card. He never went to that sushi restaurant again.

—

The near giving away of prized personal possessions was another indicator of internal stress. It was a function of Skyler's need for financial resources to fuel the appetite for drugs...

I need another eight-ball of cocaine before I run out.

...combined with the bipolar disorder's emotionally impulsive decision-making:

I must sell this keyboard now!

And the schizophrenic's poorly thought-out choice-selection:

A hundred for a keyboard valued at ten thousand? Good choice!

At a music store one day, he asked the clerk: "Hey, I've got a Roland synthesizer, top of the line, with real wood for keys. Any takers?"

"Sorry, sir, we couldn't give you much for it. You're better off taking it to a secondhand store."

"Are you sure? I'll offer it to you for a hundred."

"Hmm. Is it in good shape?"

"Like new!"

So, he sold his keyboard in desperation to a savvy customer. One hundred dollars for a keyboard that had cost him ten grand.

But I saw it for its utility and use-value, not as a treasured, priceless possession. I can part with it.

Perhaps. But he was also a slave to his passions. He needed more revenue to fuel his habits.

And then, in a fit of absence of mind, he gave all his good clothes to Goodwill and Salvation Army for nothing, just to get the monkey off his back. He thought that it would be good karma for him if he did God's work. Besides, he could not keep lugging that stuff around. It was quite a varied and eclectic mix of threads.

Man, this stuff is just heavy!

A few of them were overboard designer $5,000 Armani custom-tailored suits, purchased in Beverly Hills. Some others were significantly less expensive, but still pricey, $2,000 off-the-rack suits that had required some alterations.

I loved these suits. Maybe somebody else can use them.

Many other "Made in China" suits costing $200 apiece in inexpensive polyester-rayon fabric were just that — cheap suits that appealed to Skyler because of the pattern of the fabric, patterns he was hard-pressed to find anywhere else — chalk stripes, windowpanes, wide pinstripes. As well, Skyler gravitated toward wide-leg, straight-leg pants, giving each whole suit an attractive drape of fabric that flattered his figure and made the whole ensemble look wicked. He didn't care where they were made or what type of fabric they were. In many cases he was just looking for a type of look. As he sat in jeans and sweatshirt outside the Goodwill store:

No longer, I guess! Bon voyage!

He gifted his collection of CDs and CD mixer to Reggie for another snort of blow. Reggie gave so little in return, and he didn't even know how to mix CDs (although he listened to electronic dance music). Nor did he care how much painstaking labor went into collecting the right CDs to mix with. Skyler almost wanted to cry when he made the transaction for so

little, but he was not himself, and his sense of judgment was impaired.

In a final swan song, Skyler sold his BMW 325i
for peanuts to a used car salesman. Skyler just
wanted to get rid of it, so long as it provided money
for his drug habit. The salesman was not pushy at all,
did not use pressure tactics, and did not even try to
con him. Actually, it was the other way around:
Skyler pressed the guy to buy it, forced the issue on
him, and sold it at a fire sale price: $500.

The salesman actually said, "What're you trying
to push on me, man?"

"Why, nothing, sir. I just need the money."
Skyler shifted from foot to foot.

"What's wrong with it?" The salesman's eyes
grew half-closed.

"Nothing's wrong with it. Did you see the
CARFAX?"

"Yeah, I guess I'm in the clear. How about five
hundred, right?"

"Yup."

"All right, here it is." He pulled out five hundred-
dollar bills from a wad as thick as his fist. Skyler eyed
the wad like a vulture eyes carrion.

"Thank you, sir. Here are the keys."

It was indeed a nice car. He was sad to see it go.

Now he no longer had a place where he could sleep. He could not go anywhere he wanted to. But to comfort himself bitterly, at least he did not have to put premium gas in it all the time. Truth be told, he was experimenting with regular unleaded toward the end.

Well, no bothering about that anymore...

⎯⎯

To do a favor for a "friend," Skyler volunteered to transport an ounce of marijuana for Reggie to another part of Hollywood: Sunset Boulevard and Fairfax Avenue. He took the bus. But when he got off, he could not focus on his mission. Instead, he was famished. His hunger gnawed at his empty stomach and overrode any other priority he possessed at that moment. That was all he could think of, so he went to the local 7-11. It was ten in the morning, he had a hangover, and he was broke, so he intended to eat for free, and no one was going to stop him.

He spied a Twinkie pastry. Hmm, good! Unzipping his backpack, he put a couple of packages behind the laptop and zipped up, unthinkingly. As he headed for the door, he heard yelling and screaming. He had his raver lid on and wore a pair of sunglasses to hide his identity.

"Thief! You! Thief!" The rather athletic clerk, a Central Asian man in his twenties, jumped over the counter and placed Skyler in a viselike grip. He struggled to break free.

Just at that moment, two police officers walked in — one skinny, the other heavyset. They were there to grab donuts and coffee, and they were not in a good mood because the morning represented a long day of dealing with irate citizens and dangerous criminals.

They noticed the commotion.

"He is a thief!" screamed out the clerk in a thick accent.

"What did he take?" The officers barked out the question, no nonsense.

The clerk shouted at the officers agitatedly, "A pastry from the shelf. I saw him take it and put it in his bag!"

Without saying anything, Skyler handed over the backpack to the beefier officer. He was scared about the Twinkies.

"Oh, what have we here!" the tough-guy officer exclaimed.

He pulled out, not a Twinkie, but the plastic bag with an ounce of marijuana.

Oh, fuck me!

What happened next was a stream-of-conscience so blindingly fast it stuck in Skyler's mind long afterward. The discomfort of his hands cuffed behind his back, the smug sneer of the clerk as Skyler the bad guy was taken away, his head carefully placed under the hood of the backseat of the squad card for a trip to the precinct, a special office where his fingers were inked, and then another room with equipment where his handsome mug was photographed.

———

Skyler was thrown unceremoniously behind bars, where he would wait for an eternity.

His three other bunkmates were all nonwhite: one black, one Hispanic, one Asian.

Skyler took the unoccupied lower bed.

The opposite bottom bunkmate sneered, "Hey, white boy. Why you in here? Don't your people got the money to get your ass out?"

The other bunkmate, opposite top, snidely commiserated, "Don't worry. His mommy and daddy got it all fixed so he'll be out soon — but only after we deal with him! El Diablo?"

There was no immediate response from El Diablo to fill the conversational void. That guy occupied the bed directly above Skyler. But there was an answer, more or less. A dull, repetitive thudding came from the top bed, then liquid started to flow and pour, on all sides, from all directions!

Oh my God, the guy is urinating from the top bunk, and it's trickling down!

In a panic, Skyler rushed out of his bunk bed and stood on the common space between the two bunk beds, grabbed the prison bars, and screamed, "GET ME OUTTA HERE!" Meanwhile, the other three inmates whooped it up and hollered their approval.

Even the police officer patrolling the hallway guffawed at Skyler's predicament. "Yeah, you go, Diablo. You got 'em!"

"I told you I'd get that lily white cocksucker, O.G.!"

"You washed him out, you motherfuckin' Triad!"

But eventually, they cycled these prisoners through. Once Skyler secured the opposite top bunk, he thought to himself:

Not a bad gig! Three square meals a day, a roof over my head, and a bed to sleep in.

The only thing that bothered him was the lack of change of clothes and a shower facility. But what did he expect? This was not a hotel. He actually might get comfy here for now.

No sooner was he getting comfortable with these three perks, and getting much needed sleep, when he woke up on the frigid, damp, mildewy floor. He had fallen off his bed. The cell was like being inside a refrigerator.

He started to mumble to himself, "I hate myself. I hate my life. I want to die."

Then he heard, "Skyler Jones!" An officer boomed his name and swung open the cell door. Somebody wearing civilian clothes at one end of the hall motioned him over. Unbeknownst to him, the District Attorney had given orders to the warden to depopulate the jails. The D.A. was so worried about jail overcrowding that he ordered the release of those prisoners who had committed the pettiest of crimes, starting with the misdemeanors, including possession of marijuana without intent to sell.

NOVEMBER - WEEK 4

As he put this sojourn in the criminal justice system behind him, Skyler stopped by the will-call window to see the warden's assistant. He picked up his wallet with $27 cash, iPhone with 40-percent battery life, and his backpack containing his laptop with 23-percent battery life left, a twin-pack of Twinkies, 35 cents in a small Ziploc, and no pot.

Must have confiscated it. I'm in one hell of a shit storm from Reggie now!

Once outside, with his phone he hit Reggie up as the lender of last resort.

"Yo, Reggie! What's going on?" That same sad plaintive wail transmitted through the bandwidth.

"Nothing. Where ya been? You kinda disappeared." Skyler could not tell what mood Reggie was in.

"Oh, I got in a little bit of trouble."

There was an exhale of air on Reggie's side. "What do you mean?"

"Oh, I got arrested for the pot and for stealing."

"You WHAT?! You IDIOT! What happened to the pot?" Skyler did not appreciate the dressing-down, nor the singular attention placed on the pot.

"The police nabbed it. Sorry, man, I know it was yours. I'll earn it back, I promise."

"That's a few hundred dollars' worth in that ounce, fool!"

"Yeah, man. I'm sorry. I'll make it up to you. Can you pick me up from jail downtown?"

"Me? Pick you *up?* From *jail?* Are you out of your goddamn mind? No way, dude. Figure a ride out for yourself, you loser! And how the hell are you going to make this up to me?"

"I mean, can you Uber me a ride out of here?"

Click.

So, four years of college hanging out together, one month partying together, and nearly $10,000 later. And no friendship whatsoever. No loyalty. No connections. Nothing. Skyler was deeply pained by this, his misaligned friend network, torn to shreds. Finally, it dawned on him:

I have not been thinking clearly, and my feelings can't be trusted.

As soon as he had made the drug connection to Reggie, he had gone down the wrong, dark path, befriending someone who never truly cared about him. Reggie's commitment to him was lighter than air. Now the realization weighed heavily on Skyler.

I'm way deep, up to my neck. Can I swim back to shore against a riptide current?

Skyler's attention turned to his wallet.

Wait, wait, wait...!

He pulled out a credit card that he didn't notice before. He looked up the balance and limit and found $68 credit left.

It's going to be close.

The amount of the Uber from the jail to 1776 N. Sycamore Avenue in Hollywood was $48.95. He ordered the ride on his phone and waited. He trembled in the gloomy, overcast late November weather.

He arrived an hour later, outside the dragon's lair. Still unsure what to do, Skyler paced back and forth on the concrete. Then, in what he considered his only, best move, he called Reggie on the intercom just outside the main entrance. *Buzz, buzz, buzz...* finally, connection.

"Who's this?" Hostility and paranoia colored the voice.

"Reg, it's me, Sky. You know, your friend?" The ingratiation dripped all over Skyler's pitiful fawning.

Reggie became even more confrontational. "Why are you here, man? You're broke, ain't you?"

"Hey, I just need some help, please!" Skyler rocked anxiously from one leg to the other. He had to go to the bathroom.

"Yo, you loser, get lost!" *Bam!* Disconnected.

Just then, somebody walked through the front door, and Skyler followed that person inside. He clambered up to the third floor and rapped on Reggie's door. Jeanne answered the door. A look of disgust, scorn, and disbelief covered her cold and distant face, making it doubly painful for Skyler to see her good looks reacting to his presence like that.

Apparently, word had gotten around. He spied Josie expressing sympathy and concern when she saw him come in. Her reaction pained him in a manner opposite to Jeanne's. To Jeanne, he felt guilt. To Josie, he felt shame.

Why can't I get myself together? Why am I worse off now than I was before? What did I do to deserve this?

Then he looked at Lucifer reclining in his leather-backed chair. Skyler pleaded, "Hey, man, I have to use your bathroom." Reggie rolled his eyes.

Once finished, Skyler began to stammer. Out of desperation and in dire straits, he spoke up. "Reggie, I need money."

Reggie snorted, "You need money? Why are you telling me?"

"Because you are my homeboy, man. Can you hook me up?" The street slang failed to register any compassion.

"Muhaha, muhaha!" Reggie cackled like a hyena, his derisive laughter echoing off and through the mean streets of Hollywood, throughout all of Los Angeles, throughout all of the Southland.

Reggie had finally broken the back of this one-time popular party animal simply by plying his trade, forcing Skyler to grovel at his feet. Jeanne, too, started to giggle sardonically, so glad that the only person who had once gotten between her and Reggie was falling apart in a very open, embarrassingly public manner.

However, Josie was not laughing. While the two others were expressing their triumphant glee, her face showed grave concern. God knows he had spent a significant fortune in a small period of time. Josie had watched, dispassionately, the number and type of dollar bills that had been exchanged over the last four weeks, and she knew the figure was well into the thousands. Why were the other two kids throwing Skyler under the bus to save their own skin?

"Hey, guys, this isn't funny. I mean he might find this very upsetting." Josie mentioned this while gesturing compassion with her hands.

"What, are you taking his side?" Reggie's face expressed a grimace of contempt and scorn.

One thing, too, that was unspoken but evident was that Skyler had never once tried to interest Josie in hard drugs. Perhaps he was selfish and wanted all of the product to himself. But he also might have been protecting Josie from his very own peer pressure. Something in his loud silence made Josie want to reach out to him in his most desperate hour.

"Please, Reggie, any bit of money would help. Please!" Skyler pleaded with clasped hands as he fell on his knees. Tears streamed down his cheeks, onto his dirty T-shirt full of holes. At this act of total submission, Jeanne sneered in triumph, and Josie held back her tears in horror.

Just then, out of all this extravagant display, Reggie had something like a change of heart.

"Yo, Skyler, come here." Reggie waved him over and to the side.

Skyler followed, still on his knees.

Quietly, Reggie offered some sympathy. "Here's a nickel bag of pot. If you want money, you have to sell this to your own customers out on the street. No cash from me, get it? Hey, don't get high on your own supply, fool!" He then pushed Skyler back to the two ladies, who were sitting on the couch behind the coffee table. "And one last thing. Before you sell it, I want you to take this camcorder and" — he paused, resuming with great gusto — "make a porno of you and Josie." Reggie pointed to her, then to Skyler. "Right here, right now, in front of us."

Reggie nodded his head toward Jeanne, then looked back at Skyler. "It's gotta be at least ten minutes long, showing every possible position. I want to see missionary, doggy-style, anal, blowjob, butt-munching. You name it, you two gotta do it. And I get the rights to keep it for distribution everywhere. Ha! 'Skyler and Josie sittin' in a tree. F-U-C-K-I-N-G.' Now get to it, you two. NOW!"

Reggie and Jeanne high-fived each other, shrieking with laughter and declaring victory.

Skyler looked down and away in despair while Reggie chortled at this corrupted nursery rhyme.

<hr>

Now it was Josie's turn to be demeaned and degraded. She shook her head while glancing at Skyler and slowly backing up. Everything about her face — eyes, nose, mouth, ears, everything — was characterized by terror.

But this was the very last straw for Skyler, who had been tapped deep inside himself, starting way down from the deepest of depths, like the black and blue of the ocean itself.

I have hit absolute rock bottom. My mental illness rages unchecked, and my drug abuse destroys myself. I have psychosis. I suffer from mood disorder. I snort

*cocaine, and I take ecstasy. If I want to rebound, I
have to ask myself, 'WHAT MAN AM I?'*

As Reggie and Jeanne continued to shriek in
laughter and Josie continued to give up ground,
Skyler realized how desperate the hour was. Only
through his desire to gain the glory for defending a
blushing woman's honor and life would he be the
man whom he had, until now, been running away
from, for so long.

This was not Skyler on drugs but a deeply
submerged and sober Skyler who just now had
surfaced for the first time in a whole month. That
was the powder keg for launching action. At first,
quietly but definitively, almost in a whisper, Skyler
said, "No." Then, more forcefully and with less
restraint, he repeated, "No!" Afterward, snarling and
with great gusto, he declared, "No!" With all the
yelling he could muster, he insisted, "NO!" Finally,
he screamed out loud, with frightening lack of
control, "Nooooooo!"

From the kneeling position, he lobbed the
camcorder in Josie's direction, where it landed on the
couch harmlessly next to her. Momentarily, he
turned to Josie, who had the most quizzical look on
her face, as if to say, "I am interested! I am curious! I

am fascinated! Tell me more! More! More!" And
that was all the seriously playful ribbing that Skyler
needed.

With superhuman rage, he got off his knees,
rubbed dry his wet eyes, wiped his face, and then
straightened up. There was a madman's glint in his
determined eyes. The three other individuals in the
room quietly went to "hush" mode. Almost impossible to believe, but he took one side of that heavy
coffee table, lifted it up with all 5'9" and 150 pounds
of himself that had not yet wasted away, and thrust
the side end-over-end, upending it and barely
missing Jeanne in the process. She nearly fell over
herself in a panic to get out of the way, while all the
powders carefully lined up in rows were displaced,
leaving a white dusty fog in the air and a white,
powdered-sugar-like coating on the floor. The foggy
air and the powdery coating must have been valued
at over a thousand dollars. Now it was just one big,
sloppy mess.

But what made the damage to the powders
irrevocable was the glass top of the coffee table that
had crashed heavily on itself, now upside-down, with
the full weight of the wooden frame hemming it all
in. Spiderweb fractures covered the floor where the
glass panels had been shattered. The combination of

dangerous shards with powdery white coating made both unusable. One thing was for certain: it would be one hell of a cleanup job.

With his current display of goods destroyed, Reggie was now the object of destruction, as well. "But? But? But?" He stammered from the ramifications of losing so many goods and so much property. But no time to deliberate! In a state of adversity, danger, and weakness, Skyler reached over and grabbed Reggie from his sitting position by the collar, hauled him up, stood him up straight, cocked a fist back, and launched a right hook, *BAM!* square on Reggie's nose. There was something about this sequence of events that made it run in slow motion, as if Skyler was just taking his sweet time. But he was just being steadily deliberate and steadfastly methodical. He knew there was time to spare to ensure that the Dragon was vanquished.

Reggie fell on his back and landed on the hard uncarpeted floor as he howled with fear, shock, and pain. There was blood everywhere: all over the floor, the furniture, the upended coffee table, mixed in with the powders, and on the top of the dealer's shirt.

As blood spurted every which way from his nostrils, Reggie tried to gather himself up with both arms off the floor. Then he looked in horror as Skyler approached him again, saying menacingly, "You're not real, you're not real, you're not real." These were the very same comments Skyler had made to Reggie but had been punished for earlier in their relationship.

Skyler stood over the criminal and delivered a half-dozen more telling blows to his head. Each time the dealer's skull bounced off the floor, Reggie pleaded pitifully, "Please! I beg you! No more!" It was like at the end of a sold-out U.F.C. fight, when the referee mercifully calls an end to the cage fighting to protect the defeated fighter from permanent damage. Except, there was no referee here to keep the fight civil. Reggie lay prone on the floor, knocked unconscious. After making sure his victim would stay on the ground, Skyler turned his attention to Jeanne, who could not believe what she had just seen: Reggie, her king, humiliated, and bloodied. And that court jester? Grimly homicidal, no longer in the mood. And she, the queen? She was about to be...*what?*

Skyler approached, and with the force of a madman, he hocked a huge loogie, cleared his throat, and emptied his nostrils. He collected all the ooze, spit, mucus, and bile he could muster. He grabbed Jeanne by the shoulders, growled his pleasure, and got close in to her face, so close that he could have kissed her. She started to wail like a petulant child and wore a look of terror and protest, as if to say, "Tell me no more! NO MORE! NO MORE!" But Skyler was dead set on defacing Jeanne with spit.

Just then, Josie came from behind him, hugged him close, and gently pulled him away, saying, "It's okay, Skyler. It's okay. It's over, it's over." Josie hushed Skyler gently and disengaged him from spitting any spit-salvos at Jeanne. He trembled with fighting spirit, sweat all over his body, his pulse sky-high.

Josie urged him, "Stop, stop, stop. That's enough! Okay, that's enough, Sky! That's enough!" She pulled him back firmly, putting her hands on his arms to release their death-grip on Jeanne.

Skyler complied as Jeanne dropped to the floor, crying, Josie continued, "That's enough, Skyler. I get it. I get it. Let it go."

Josie was in a tough bind here. Skyler was her newfound hero, but Jeanne was her old-time friend. What he did to Reggie made its point loud and clear. The same action did not have to be extended to Jeanne, to whom Josie expressed some vestige of loyalty.

As Skyler released Jeanne from his grip, his arm

came in contact with a bulge on Josie's right side. In his dimly enlightened rage, Skyler thought:

Does Josie pack heat?

It just was not clear if she had a concealed-carry permit. As Josie disengaged, the bulge disappeared. Skyler dropped both arms, unimpeded, to their sides. Everything returned to normal. Josie held onto whatever remaining friendship she had with Jeanne, while Skyler said, with his arms now at his sides, "Nothing personal, Jeanne. Don't take it personally."

After nearly suffering catastrophe, Jeanne completely froze. One of her formerly slitty eyes was now bug-eyed. She looked over at the prone Reggie, who had by now regained consciousness. As if reading each other's mind, they both made a beeline for the bathroom.

For Josie and Skyler, they could both hear and see it all:

Reggie shoved Jeanne aside as he charged at the mirror. "Move, dammit, move! I have to see myself!"

She was worried about him. "Just let me see your face!"

"Why? Dammit, I've got blood everywhere!"

"Where are the cotton pads? The cotton pads! Let me turn on some hot water!"

"Get your goddamn head out of my mirror!"

"Oh, no, if people saw you now..."

———

That manic rage subsided. Skyler seemed to wake up as if from a bad dream, as if he were no longer in a nightmare fighting a demon. That crazed glint in his eyes had disappeared, and humanity returned to his dilated pupils. His chest heaved, although he had not run the hundred-meter dash.

What just happened?

With a sad, forlorn look at Josie, Skyler said to her, "I didn't want you to witness that. I can't be here anymore." His previously sluggish brain suddenly slid onto a well-greased track.

Back to reality!

He rushed for the door but not before grabbing his backpack.

Josie yelped, "Skyler, wait!" and was torn

momentarily between tending to Jeanne, on one hand, and running off with Skyler, on the other. She looked around — red blood, dusted powders, broken glass — then she listened. Wailing and yelling were coming from the bathroom. Something held her back from running out of the room for dear life. She felt for them. But what about Skyler? But then, *what about him?* He was a mess too. She had given it everything to hold him back from defacing Jeanne, and the way he had attacked Reggie was borderline homicidal. Josie kept trying to reconcile the Skyler she had known for almost a month with the Skyler she had observed for not even an hour. He had almost killed Reggie. And nearly traumatized Jeanne.

Then, she decided.

She gathered her belongings, went out the door, headed down the hallway, flew down to the first floor, took off outside down the flight of stairs, and hurtled down to the sidewalk. The streetlights provided partial identification, but the sun had set hours ago, and her hopes for finding Skyler deflated as she scanned Sycamore Boulevard, north and south and back, and over onto the opposite side of the street, where apartment buildings as varied as people's faces registered no human presence.

Skyler was nowhere to be found.

Looking at her watch ("It's ten o'clock!"), she realized he could be anywhere by now. Josie went to her navy Chevy Impala parked just up the street on N. Sycamore, dropped all her stuff inside the passenger's side front seat, and drove home to North Hollywood, without her beau and sans Jeanne.

Modern medical science affirms a *virtuous circle* of talk therapy and psychotropic medication to treat mental illnesses. If pursued vigorously, the approach leaves much hope for the future. At this point, Skyler dimly recognized that. But had Skyer's ship already sailed? Had he given too much ground, much too soon?

The answer? It is never too late. One starts by addressing the physical origins of the disorder's symptoms. Psychotropic medications target the brain cells with additional amounts of beneficial chemicals — to help elevate mood, for example. By understanding how these chemicals work, the psychiatrist can properly medicate patients, sending the symptoms into remission. Skyler had not digested that information.

I didn't give Dr. Wilson much of a chance, I guess.

Skyler's feelings of guilt and shame were almost too much for him to bear. He winced at the memory of himself giving Dr. Wilson a difficult time.

In a similar vein, talk therapy with a patient could unearth underlying conflicts and hidden traumas in the patient's life. Therefore, a psychologist can help the patient overcome whatever mental blocks to growth there might be and thereby lead to new uncharted vistas for the patient.

Until now, Skyler did not get it.

I guess I didn't get very far with Ms. Martinez, huh?

A deep, dark gloom descended on him when he thought of how little he had achieved with Ms. Martinez, when he could have made the most of it.

For those combining partying (the flipside of therapy) with self-medication (the flipside of psychotropic medication), the chances are slim to none that recovery will come emerge. Babbling incoherently to self-absorbed partygoers is likely to be met with indifference. And even serious listeners in altered states of mind cannot generate helpful feedback. Meanwhile, snorting various powders without knowledge of their devastating downsides is a game of Russian roulette. For Skyler, this "self-medication" was an inaccurate and inconsistent approach to targeting one's brain chemistry. The combined approach created a *vicious cycle* that, if left unchecked, could lead to brain damage, social isolation, and suicidal ideation. And those sad outcomes were exactly where Skyler was headed.

▭

DECEMBER
AMAZING GRACE

DECEMBER

DECEMBER - WEEK 1

It was ten o'clock in the evening. Skyler sprinted down N. Sycamore Avenue as if his life depended on it. He was not sure how much "muscle" Reggie had to avenge himself with. Maybe the dealer toted a gun, one which Skyler had never seen. But he had not thought of that in the middle of his "outburst."

After a while he slowed down, totally gassed, and bent over, hands on knees, to catch his short, smoke-addled breath, coughing and sputtering. He looked around, no longer manic, but he had no clue where he was. The street signs were alien.

Where is Sycamore?

All he knew was that he had passed the glitz of

Hollywood Boulevard way back to get some cover in a dark side street. But at least he knew he was alive.

He decided to get his bearings.

Oh, right! I've got a backpack with me.

Grabbing the wallet from the backpack, he took inventory of it first.

Twenty-seven bucks, a debit card connected to a bank account with nothing in it, a maxed-out credit card, and my driver's license.

He searched his pockets.

Thirty-five cents in my right pocket. My phone charged to thirty percent in my left pocket.

Next, it was more from the backpack.

My laptop with fifteen-percent charge and a twin-pack of Twinkies.

That was everything he had. Little wonder. He had frivolously spent and frittered away his entire life savings of ten grand. Thinking of survival, he opened the stale Twinkies package and tried to get some nourishment out of it.

"A sugar high," he thought out loud. "At least I got the Twinkies for free." He laughed bitterly.

He wandered the streets of Hollywood for one terrifying night. He was in good company here among criminals, crazies, homeless, addicts, runaways, and tourists. But as the sun rose, he heard something like voices.

Oh no, Here they come again.

Such utter, unimpeded anguish.

Is it really voices?

In his enfeebled state, his hold on reality was tenuous. After all, when in the past he was even the least bit disturbed, he had no hold on reality. But in this reality, the sound he heard was music!

Is it just in my reality that I hear the music? Or is the music in everybody's reality, including my own?

He needed to know more about this music — music that was fashioned like no other, timeless and timely. He wandered into the building where the music was coming from, a Southern Baptist church. He was raised Presbyterian, so he knew there were regional differences but all Christian, nevertheless. When he was younger, Skyler admired his parents for his religious upbringing.

Only a makeshift church, not a huge one, would answer my pleas for deliverance.

A choir was singing the music to the accompaniment of a pianist on a Wurlitzer. A pastor conducted the ensemble. Seeing Skyler, he smiled and motioned him inside. Skyler practically fell inside the church and collapsed into one of the pews. Yet he assumed a respectful and dignified demeanor, his back straight, his head bent forward, his hands clasped together in front of him, listening to each line sung with glorious passion, with religious love, with the Lord's desire, with Platonic romance.

The music spoke to him. What did he hear?

I hear in the chord changes an undeserved kindness from a higher power. In the melody, I hear the sound of spiritual salvation. I hear in the lyrics a triumphant overcoming of adversity. In each verse, the words are exhibiting a transformative power away from sin. In each and every lyric, there is a source of comfort.

This was music like no other! He made a note on his laptop about this music and its lyrics, intending to retrieve them from publicly available sources.

There is no copyright protection on this one, I'm sure!

After the last verse was sung, Skyler forced himself back on his feet, dried his tears on his T-shirt, bowed gratefully to the choir, and then waved to the pastor, who waved right back.

———

It was eight o'clock in the morning. In what could only be called a life-changing moment, Skyler reached out for a lifeline. With his phone low on juice, he called a familiar number.

"Hello?" A friendly tone.

"Hi, Ms. Martinez?" His hand that held the phone trembled.

"Yes. Who am I speaking with?" It was a bright warble that made her voice attractive.

A somewhat inquisitive impulse took over. "Oh,

this is Skyler Jones. Do you remember me? We stopped talking about a month ago."

"I get it, Skyler." She sounded sad. "How are you? Everything okay? You left treatment without saying anything." Her concern seeped into her voice, despite the memory of Skyler's abrasiveness during their last meeting.

"Yes, I am sorry for that. I have been dropping the ball on a lot of people lately. But I am ready to go back into treatment. I realize now that you were only trying to help me." Skyler let the walls come down, and he started to cry quietly.

"I am guessing times have been difficult for you, this last month or so. Have you spoken to Dr. Wilson about your change of heart?"

"No, but if you and he are still part of the same treatment team, then I would like to work with him again too. Please." He clasped both hands together, with the phone in the middle.

"Okay, then. When do you want to have your first appointment?" She had her planner out in front of her.

"Do you have later today, like this morning?"

"As a matter of fact, I do. That would be ten o'clock with me, followed by eleven o'clock with Dr. Wilson. We reserved that for you, and your Uncle

Frank said he would pay in case you returned to treatment. I will call him to let him know you have resumed sessions. Let's get started later today. My office, please." She added, "And I won't mind at all if you call me Eleanor."

"Thank you, thank you, thank you, Eleanor." He dried his tears on his T-shirt.

"You're welcome, Skyler."

<hr>

It was half-past eight in the morning. Skyler reached out again, to another lifeline.

"Hello?" A deep, baritone voice. Skyler knew that one.

"Uncle Frank, it's Skyler." He tried to sound adult and grown-up.

"Skyler! How are you? Where are you?" Frank asked frantically.

"I'm okay. Look, I want to apologize to you and Aunt Nancy for my past behavior. Everything about it, including all of it after graduation. You're right, I needed more help, and more professional help, than you could provide me. I hope you will accept my apology, and forgive me, Uncle Frank." Now Skyler got it finally — a 180-degree change in attitude.

"Well, Skyler, I appreciate it. I really do. You know, as your uncle, and speaking for Nancy, it is really encouraging to hear those words straight from you. It seemed that for the longest time we couldn't even have a decent conversation lasting longer than one minute without a shouting match erupting."

"It started with me, Uncle Frank. It started with me, I know it. I was very disrespectful to you, and I scared the bejesus out of Aunt Nancy. That's not how family members are supposed to treat each other."

"You know, Skyler, we just got a call from Eleanor Martinez and Ralph Wilson about you reaching out to them to restart the talk therapy and "psych meds." And we treat your apology doubly sincerely this time because of that. It was prearranged that we would resume payment of medical services for you once you returned to treatment. Again, we want you to focus on your mental health recovery and your sobriety from drugs and alcohol. That's what we learned about you over the past couple of months, that your diagnosis is co-occurring disorder, not simply mental illness. That has got to be more than twice as debilitating. And you know what? At this point, I'm just glad you're alive." Frank slumped in the chair he was sitting in, knowing that he had underestimated what Skyler was going through.

"It is a very tough diagnosis, I admit, Uncle Frank. But actually, now that I know what I'm dealing with, that really is half the battle. I know what I have to do — mental health recovery, and abstinence from drugs and alcohol, together. That's not impossible. Others, I'm sure, have done it. So can I!" Skyler sat upright in his chair, knowing that perhaps he was a mustard seed, the smallest of the seeds in the plant kingdom, but which can grow to one of the mightiest trees there are in the forest.

"Well, I suppose others have done it, but you have a lot of advantages too. You have family, you're intelligent, you're educated, you have the lived experience of the illness, and you have friends —" Skyler's uncle was on a roll.

"Maybe not too many friends, Uncle Frank. I think I burned a lot of bridges, actually."

"Well, let time determine that. Now you and I really struggled to come to an agreement about your trust fund which, again, I was placed executor of until you came of age. You recall?" Frank wanted to make this right.

"Yes, sir."

"I want you to tell me your financial situation. Just straight up, just the facts. Okay?"

"Okay. So, I had ten thousand in savings from allowances over the years, my summer jobs, campus UCLA library job, and the Raleigh Studios job. I spent it all. I spent it frivolously. I frittered it all away. But I also lived on it because I was too incapacitated to work. And I sold most of my possessions for money. The CDs and CD mixer, my Yamaha keyboard, the BMW, my clothes..."

"Okay, Skyler, you know what? I really, really, wish I had been more charitable to you two months ago. Look, let's help each other out. I want you to come see me now. Right now. Are you in the area?"

"I'm in Hollywood somewhere."

"Okay, look, I want you to get an Uber to our house. I'll order it. I would rather we speak in person." This time, in the interests of kindness and generosity, Frank was all business.

———

Thirty minutes later, at nine o'clock, Uncle Frank swung the door wide open. There was Skyler, dirty, sweaty, smelly, having wasted away thirty-five pounds, down to 155. His dry drugged-out eyes had trouble focusing in the frosty winter weather. His skin took on a sallow shade, and he had a month's worth of beard growth. But his otherwise untouched backpack gleamed in the sun. If his uncle looked taken aback by Skyler's appearance, he did not let on.

"Come on in, Skyler." True enough, he had never seen his nephew so strung out like this. But now, he let on. "First of all, go upstairs, shower and shave, and get a change of clothes from the dresser in your room."

Skyler felt so dirty and grimy that he didn't remotely consider Uncle Frank's words as off-putting nor as overly imposing.

He went upstairs. Nothing had changed. In the dresser, the same old socks, same old underwear, same old T-shirts, same old jeans, and same old sweatshirts. But Skyler valued them at a price far beyond any standard he had judged them by prior to his disappearance. Before his .trip to hell and back, he had seen brands: Polo Ralph Lauren, Michael Kors, and Giorgio Armani... Now he saw fabrics: cotton, wool, polyester, and linen. He got it: form follows function.

Too bad he had not had the good manners — and

vanity — to get a haircut. He could not spare the expense.

Skyler came back down thirty minutes later.

Uncle Frank began with, "Let's have a seat in the living room. Skyler, I want us to meet periodically, let's say once a month, okay? We'll have dinner together and talk about how things are going. And in return, I will provide you with financial support. Do you have access to your bank account?"

"Yes, my debit card should do it."

"Okay. Starting forward — and I will get this in writing for you — but for now I will wire you some emergency funds, ten thousand, to replace what you lost, so you can get by for now, into your bank account. There has to be a solemn vow on your part, Skyler. We need you to focus solely on mental health recovery and sobriety from drugs and alcohol. Okay? But let's remember, we need you to live on your own. How about you stay with us through December. But come the New Year, we can't hold your hand. You need to be independent. Of course, you may stay for a few nights whenever you are visiting. But that's it."

Suddenly, Skyler's eyes focused, his back straightened, and he heaved a sigh of relief. "Uncle Frank, you have my word, as an honorable man, that I will do everything in my human power not to fall through the cracks again. I will engage in transparent and accountable conduct, and I will spend the money you provide me in a manner that is right, just, and fair."

Skyler grimaced slightly and bent his head as he felt the awful weight of his word and the burden of his honor on his back and shoulders.

"Thank you, Skyler. You have no idea what those words mean to me. And trust me, you and I will discuss steps moving forward. Okay? So..." Uncle Frank shifted some papers on the dining room table around and continued, "...by ten o'clock or so, the money will be available. Go ahead and check on your end. Let me know if it does not pop up. Work on getting your life back together, young man. We love you."

"I love you and Aunt Nancy too!" Skyler's hoarse voice was raspy with tears and sweat, as if he had resisted saying it all along and had surrendered to say it. But he meant it.

"Now when are you seeing Eleanor and Ralph next?"

"At ten and eleven this morning. Can you please get me an Uber to Larchmont Village?"

"No problem. Let's go order it now."

———

At ten o'clock in Larchmont Village, Eleanor Martinez and Skyler Jones explored his situation together. Why all the drug abuse in the recent past? Something had been motivating it as an escape from reality. After all, it was only since Skyler's graduation from UCLA that he had called up Reggie. What it was, Ms. Martinez did not know, but Skyler might be "sitting" on the reason, as if it were right under his nose. There was a hidden trauma that generated internal conflict and that prevented Skyler from progress and growth.

"I remember a time with my sister, Emily. I am scared to talk about her ever since my family died. Because I feel bad about her."

"Can you remember the setting?"

"Yeah. It was ten o'clock. It was a school night. Mom and Dad were out on movie night together. Emily and I had gone to bed. We were both in high school. But I couldn't get to sleep. One time, I went to Emily's room...this is tough." Skyler bent over and put his head in his hands.

"Go on. You are doing fine."

He straightened out and forced himself to look squarely at Ms. Martinez. "She was sleeping, and ... I kind of jumped on top of her...I forced my way under the covers...while I was naked...and I pulled her underwear aside and down. Then she woke up all of a sudden...looked at me...and started screaming, 'Don't Skyler, don't! Stop! Stop! Stop! What're you doing? You're my brother! No! No! No! No! No, please, no!' until I forced myself inside her. Then she started to cry."

Skyler grimaced with the pain of the memory. "Then I stopped and pulled out." He put his head in his hands. "She kept saying the same thing afterward, "I trusted you! I trusted you! I trusted you!"

"Did you feel that one of you was the victim and the other the perpetrator?" Gentle empathy filled the therapist's voice.

"Yeah. I admit I felt like the perpetrator and that she was the victim."

"That is a difficult memory to carry around with oneself. So can you tell me what happened next?" Gently, and expertly, Ms. Martinez steered the session.

"Afterwards, she went to the bathroom and turned on the light to fix up her clothes while she looked at herself in the mirror. I went to the toilet to pee, and I was laughing, as if it were funny. She had stopped screaming and had stopped crying by now. I was seventeen, while she was fifteen. That's another reason I felt like the perpetrator and she the victim. So, therefore, the voice that says, over and over, generating my feelings of shame, 'You horrible piece of shit!'"

As Skyler recalled the experience, he burst into tears of self-loathing, and he returned his head to rest in his hands. Out of compassion, Ms. Martinez asked him to push through the feelings of revulsion. She asked, "But why was it wrong rather than just simply taboo? People don't talk about these things in broad daylight, Skyler. This is the right place to talk about it. I am encouraging you to think that way. You would be surprised how often this kind of thing troubles people."

He lifted his tear-stained head from his hands. "Really?"

"You know, you were both minors at the time. You were not consenting adults. If one of you were of legal age, while the other was a minor, that might be considered statutory rape, you know. That's why there is a stigma associated with incest. Skyler, I applaud and admire your willingness to go over this difficult experience in order to get better. Let's continue on other things for the rest of the session, if you would like."

"Oh." Skyler massaged his brow, where he had a splitting headache.

"Any other voices? I think there was one that directed you to kill yourself."

"I want to do that! I just want to do away with myself. I hate myself!" He screamed out loud. He felt the labor of therapy overcoming his own resistance to getting better.

"Is that also from the same experience?"

"Yes! I think it's them, my family, you know, who want me to join them in the afterlife, in hell, in fact."

"But how would that fix things? And why would they send you to hell? And why would they be there, of all places? Many people love you, Skyler. Your Uncle Frank and Aunt Nancy, for example. Do you have any idea how many people you would hurt if you were to die by suicide? Think about it."

"I know, I know! I want to make amends, I really do. I want the drug abuse to stop. I want the voices to go away. I want my moods to even out. Maybe I'm wrong, thinking that my family wanted me to die with them. Maybe that's some other voice."

"Well, you came to the right place. Our time is up, but why don't you talk to Dr. Wilson? He has you down for thirty minutes during which you will have a lot to talk about. Tell him, to whatever extent you are comfortable, what you're feeling, what you're thinking, and go from there."

"Okay, thank you, Eleanor. I appreciate you."

"No problem, Skyler. I will talk to you next week, on Monday the seventh."

———

Skyler had Dr. Wilson at eleven o'clock in Larchmont Village, later that morning, which was the first of December. In the back of Skyler's mind, he tried to echo what Ms. Martinez had said. His treatment team cared for him, not so much because of the dire straits he was in but more so because he had the potential to recover. After all, he had achieved a 180-degree change in his attitude, from abject rejection to wholehearted acceptance. He had decided, after attempting and rejecting treatment, to give it the old college try.

The door to the doctor's office swung open, and Dr. Wilson was there to greet Skyler.

"Skyler, come on in!"

He walked on through but chose to follow the doctor to the leather couch that was assigned to the patient.

Soon they were sitting, facing each other, and the

doctor was comfortably perched on his leather chair. Skyler was all pins and needles.

"Okay, Dr. Wilson. I apologize for my terribly disrespectful behavior a month ago. It may have been the illness, but I refuse to pass the buck. I accept responsibility for my actions. Explanations, not excuses. I'm ready to try a new medication regimen." He looked at Dr. Wilson directly.

"Yes, we last talked one month ago." The doctor scanned his notes.

Skyler answered, "That's right. Yep, that's correct."

"Any drug use in the past month or so?"

"Yes. Powders. And marijuana. I threw away the Depakote and Risperdal."

"Okay, first things first. Get off the street drugs right away."

"Okay. I'm sober as of a few days ago. That's not a long time, but it's a promise. That stuff is behind me. It nearly ruined and destroyed my life. It nearly killed me. I don't want brain damage. I don't ever want to do those drugs again." Skyler wrung his hands and spoke with an air of measured urgency.

"Good. Okay, so last time my notes showed that the medications I initially placed you on did not work and gave you unacceptable side effects. That was the anti-psychotic Risperdal and the mood stabilizer Depakote. Correct?"

"Yes, that's correct," Skyler's palms got sweaty.

"You gave both a try, and we in fact went up to the full dosage in four weeks, in the month of October. You should be praised for sticking with the drugs for that long. Some of my patients don't want to take medication, so there's nothing I can do for them."

"Really?" Skyler was dumbfounded.

Who would go see a psychiatrist and not want to get medicated?

"Yes. They want to see a psychiatrist, but they do not want to take medication. You're better off already compared to them."

The doctor studied Skyler a moment, then continued, "I'm going to try something different. There is another antipsychotic we can use, Loxapine. I'm going to put you on fifty milligrams, for two weeks, and then if there are no bad side effects, I will increase the dosage to a hundred for another two weeks, over the course of this month." Dr. Wilson leaned on the armrest of his chair. "I'm going to ask you to take it at nighttime because it does make people drowsy. Does that make sense?"

"Yeah, it does. It really does." Skyler admitted this time that it did make sense.

"I can't put you on the full dosage right away. It has to be gradually entered into the bloodstream. So that would mean that in this month of December you'll begin treatment and then adjust treatment with me."

Skyler nodded in agreement. "Yes. In October you and Ms. Martinez tried very hard to work with me. In November I gave up hope. And in December..." His words trailed off.

Dr. Wilson picked up, "Now based on your allergic reaction to the Risperdal, Loxapine should be more effective, leave no side effects, and positively affect your mood, based on other patients' favorable experiences."

"Trust me, Doctor, nothing would make me happier." A big grin flashed on Skyler's face.

"You and me both! Now, the other thing is the mood stabilizer Depakote I prescribed, which gave you unacceptable weight gain. Besides, the Depakote did not give you much positive benefit." The doctor frowned. "I am going to put you on lithium, which was the first drug to be approved by the U.S. Food and Drug Administration for bipolar disorder. It's actually a naturally occurring salt."

"So, the tried and true are better than the relatively recent ones?" Skyler asked for an honest answer. He was trying to figure out for himself the rationale for trying certain substances before or over another. He wanted to be an informed patient. He wanted to be cooperative.

"It can be, Skyler, it can be. Fortunately, we have an arsenal of drugs to choose from these days. Decades ago, that wasn't the case." Dr. Wilson uncrossed his legs into a more comfortable position. "I am going to put you on five-hundred milligrams of lithium a day for two weeks, to be doubled to a thousand daily in two weeks. Again, please note that I cannot shock your system by giving you a thousand right away. Understand? It has to be increased slowly."

Skyler nodded firmly and pursed his lips.

"I will ask you to take the lithium at nighttime along with the Loxapine because it also does make people drowsy. Okay?"

Dr. Wilson scribbled out two prescriptions and extended them with an outstretched arm and a smile.

Skyler reached out, beamed a smile back, and daintily accepted the two pieces of paper.

"It makes perfect sense, Doc. Last time we talked, I didn't understand the nature of the different types of medication, the necessity of increasing dosages, and their intended effects. Now I do, even though I'm not properly medicated. I just feel a lot calmer now. One thing...?"

"Yes?"

"Will the voices inside my ahead go away?"

"Well, we'll have to see how the new medications work out, but if they do work out, then we should see a definite effect on the voices. That is what we mean when we talk about psychosis: it generates hallucinations, whether hearing things that are not there or seeing things that are not there. An antipsychotic works on the chemicals in the brain to combat those hallucinations. So that is what the Loxapine is for."

"Got it, doc, I got it. Eureka."

"Another thing, work hard in therapy with Ms. Martinez. If you can pinpoint the reasons for the voices with her, alongside you and I pinpointing the right medications to make the voices go away, then you will be in good shape."

"I get it. But I guess I had to hit rock bottom myself before I could rebound."

"Skyler, unfortunately that's part of the treatment. To be able to hang in there until rescue comes. You're starting off on the right foot, and you will do better. You have the self-motivation to get better. I see that right away. That's important. We'll talk again toward the end of the month, on the twenty-ninth."

━━━

Skyler went to the pharmacy down the main drag of Larchmont Boulevard and, with the health insurance Uncle Frank paid for, filled the prescriptions, which were handed to him in translucent plastic orange bottles in a white paper bag. Then Skyler waited outside for the Uber his uncle had ordered to get him back to their house in the Hollywood Hills.

Once at their beautiful home, Skyler spotted them sitting in the living room, He greeted them respectfully by presenting the white paper bag with both upraised arms. Noting their now-openly care-worn faces, he explained, "New medications. Different ones."

Uncle Frank nodded. Aunt Nancy stood up, stepped forward, and happily hugged Skyler tightly. "It is so good to see you, dear," she said.

Skyler was skinny again, she noticed — no protruding breasts, no protruding stomach. Snorting all those powders up his nose and curtailing his Risperdal and Depakote intake together ruined his appetite. Two months had passed, one when he tried psych-meds and talk therapy, one when he tried street drugs and endless partying. He was back to square one now. Or was he? Did he learn something from this two-month crash course in lived experience?

"All right, Skyler, we're going to have Christmas dinner on the twenty-fourth and a Christmas Day birthday party on the twenty-fifth to celebrate your birthday." Nancy's voice rang loud and clear. Reading Skyler's blank stare, she went on, "Yes, your birthday. What, did you think we forgot it?"

Wow, my birthday's December 25, 2000. If Uncle Frank and Aunt Nancy had forgotten, nobody would have known.

DECEMBER - WEEK 2

In Week One, Skyler fought the voices in his head for supremacy of the mental airwaves. The relief that Skyler felt in last week's session by trusting Eleanor Martinez was a huge, tangible first step in the right direction. Now, beginning Week Two together, they started the session at ten o'clock on the eighth of December.

"Is there anything new to report since our last meeting, Skyler?" She chewed on a pencil.

"Well, my uncle and aunt made a very generous concession since the beginning of this month, to disburse some of my trust fund which is under their supervision so that I could focus my time and energy on sobriety and recovery. I showed my respect to them." A huge grin showed up on Skyler's face.

"And how did you show your respect to them?" A smile crept on the therapist's face.

"Do you really want to know?"

"Yes! Tell me."

"I bowed to them. Deeply. Like this!" When Skyler was a young child prodigy on the piano, that was what he learned to do to show respect to his audience. But now the audience he wished to win over was his family.

"And the voices? Or voice? Are they still speaking?"

"They seem to be less invasive. They kind of come and go. They are not targeted specifically at me as they used to be previously." Skyler moved his arms this way and that, to emphasize the point. "I think that Dr. Wilson taught me that a combination of psych meds and talk therapy best handles these situations. I've only given the meds one week to kick in at the starting dosage, so I don't want to paint too rosy of a picture, but I'm willing to continue working with you, Ms. Martinez. I know that I feel a lot less like a pressure-cooker holding it in and trying so hard to forget about it. Now that I think of it, it doesn't feel so bad after all."

On the fifteenth of December, as directed by Dr. Wilson and as listed on the prescription bottle's instructions, Skyler bumped up his dosage of lithium to 1,000 mg and Loxapine to 100 mg. It was a bit of a disappointment for him, admittedly. He expected a jackpot of freshly wrought thoughts and fine-hearted feelings. But he murmured to himself with a wan smile, "I guess it doesn't work that way."

DECEMBER - WEEK 3

Then he began Week Three of therapy that morning at ten o'clock with Ms. Martinez.

"The voices have definitely diminished. They are not as loud anymore. They are fewer in number. It emerges only when I think about Emily. They do not spill over into other regions of my life."

"What do you think this change means? In other words, is there anything that was said or done that would justify the diminishment of the voices?"

"Well, I thought all along that the treatment was what brought me back. It's true that all those powders made me escape from the past, from reality, but then I was completely incapacitated by them. I could only escape for a little while, then I had to do more of them, just for the same effect. That doesn't sound too therapeutic to me."

"Mental health is a tough subject for a lot of people. Consider yourself fortunate enough that you really do want to get better, that you are doing hard work in therapy, you seem to respond well to medication, and you have a family that cares about you."

"Thank you, Eleanor."

———

On December 22, marking two weeks of an initial dosage of lithium and Loxapine, and one week of the recommended new dosage of the two, Skyler had some important news to report.

"Eleanor, the voices are gone. They no longer say, 'You horrible piece of shit. You should kill yourself.'"

"Great! You should be applauded for sticking to the medication regimen and seeing that it works. That's unusual that the medication acted so quickly."

"Well, I have to admit that there is another voice. Actually, voices."

"Can you tell me what they say?"

"Well, they are rather beautiful. They say, 'Your

secret is safe with me.' 'My lips are sealed.' 'I won't tell a soul.' 'I'll keep this between us.'"

"Wow. As a therapist I hear a lot of boring stuff, but this is interesting. Fascinating, in fact. Who do you think is saying this, and why would they say this?"

"Well, the only logical place is from Heaven and from different manifestations of my angel, Emily." He started to sob. "She is forgiving me. I thought for the longest time that it was from Hell and from my Emily the demon, and she was cursing me."

Boy, I just found religion pretty fast, huh?

Skyler rubbed his tear-stained face with his hands with a Kleenex from a dispenser on the coffee table.

━━━

At his uncle and aunt's, on the afternoon of the twenty-fifth — a Monday — an early "Christmas-Birthday" dinner was being prepared. Skyler joined Frank on the backyard patio, where the steaks were being grilled to perfection.

"Rare?" he asked Skyler while prodding the

New York Strip steak that Skyler made a beeline toward with his eyes.

"Moving! Yes, sir, please." Skyler exulted that his uncle remembered his preference for steak.

"And yours and Aunt Nancy's are well done, right?" Skyler asked in turn.

"You know it, Skyler."

Yup, Skyler had remembered too.

"By the way, we also have corn on the cob grilling, and mashed potatoes and stuffing with gravy indoors, that Aunt Nancy is making. And apple pie for dessert."

After the steaks were grilled, Frank moved the action indoors to the kitchen. There Skyler saw the potatoes mashed, stuffing heaped, and gravy heated, filling the air with smells that he had not known in months.

It was a quiet meal, where the short and shallow lines of communication were interspersed with long and meaningful periods of silence. Skyler felt that he had not tasted food before, precisely because he had taken food this good for granted. He indeed had been entitled to many things. But he had not been coddled either, especially in recent memory. Anybody who had lost his family prematurely, garnered a legiti-mate degree from a respectable college, turned the corner on mental illness, and had renounced a life of drugs and alcohol, had earned himself a first-class ticket to an easier life.

After helping clear the table and drying the dishes after dinner, Skyler looked at his watch — seven o'clock.

He suggested, "How about some musical entertainment? I want to play the piano to back up your singing, Uncle Frank. As you might have guessed, I don't have that electronic keyboard anymore. I put up the composition as a piano accompaniment on my iPad, and it goes well with voices. You and Aunt Nancy have the Steinway. That's better than any keyboard I know."

"Go ahead, Skyler. I'm curious to know what you learned over the last few months."

"Just one. But it saved my life. I'll play the instrumental part through first, then please join me. Trust me, you know it."

Skyler walked over to the Steinway, perched gracefully in the living room. He placed his iPad on the sheet music stand, sat down on the cushioned bench and rested his hands on the keyboard in familiar fashion, on a D7 chord. It continued to G major, with Skyler playing the all-too-familiar soprano melody with his ring and pinky fingers of the right hand, and with the accompanying alto voice in his thumb, index or middle finger on the right hand. And now the tenor voice was played by "fingers one through three" and bass by "fingers four and five" in the left hand, harmonizing and anchoring the right hand.

It was not too hard to play, since it started at a slow gait. Hence, it did not require virtuoso technique. And it was not overly complex in structure, since it stayed in a major key, and the chord changes remained diatonic. Still, there was something that Skyler profoundly loved about it.

Aunt Nancy went "Whoa!" with pleasure upon hearing the refrain of the music — very familiar to everybody. What was it exactly? Well, Uncle Frank rose from his seat and cleared his throat out of love of Skyler's choice of music.

"Repeat! I'll sing!" Frank exclaimed excitedly.

He boomed the first — and most famous — verse in a deep, rich baritone voice while Skyler repeated the piano part. The music reminded Skyler of being lost in Hollywood, after he had stood up for himself and his girl, Josie. He knew what the church music he heard was meant for him. And how, now, his family had taken him back, and they were helping him heal:

Amazing grace! How sweet the
sound,
that saved a wretch like me.
I once was lost, but now am found,
was blind but now I see!

A beautiful song, imbued with class and simplicity, was rich in meaning and full of life! That music in the folksy church in the heart of Hollywood had been no mistake, for sure. It meant many things on many levels to Skyler, and even though it had been played in a secular setting, it had not lost any of its original meaning. It actually meant even more now — undeserved kindness from a higher power, spiritual salvation from despair, the overcoming of grave adversity, the power of transformation into a better self, and a source of comfort from tragedy.

Nancy, who had been quietly listening from the living room's leather sofa, clapped happily at the end. Frank beamed with a huge happy smile. Skyler felt unadulterated happiness for the first time in a long time.

And immediately afterward, the young man revealed something in his vulnerability. "Uncle Frank and Aunt Nancy, you're the only family I've got left."

"And you, Skyler, are the only family we have. We think of you as our child, son. Let's continue to make peace in the family, Skyler, from now on. Now, how about another slice of apple pie?"

***

On December 29, at the fifth meeting of Skyler with his therapist and two whole weeks with the higher dosage of the medication, there was interesting news to report.

"Okay, Skyler. Where would you like to start today?"

"Oh, I don't know. I think we should focus on any more traumas and conflicts I may have."

"That's an excellent place to start, Skyler," she said.

"It seemed the voices have gone away, even the angelic ones. I wonder whether I need to focus on Emily and me anymore. She's not really dead so long as I remember her. And now I want to remember her instead of trying to forget her. Or what happened between me and her." Skyler shifted around in his seat and looked down.

"Somebody once told me that to 'forgive and remember' is a noble sentiment. After all, we cannot forget something that generates trauma or causes internal conflict. Maybe I should ask for forgiveness from Emily, from the grave." Skyler began to cry.

"Keep going, Skyler. You're doing wonderfully." His therapist offered kind words of encouragement.

Skyler continued while sniffling, "I guess asking a dead person for forgiveness is not possible, but those horrible voices of mine went away. At first, I was stuck. I was torn apart by internal conflict. Those voices nearly destroyed me. Then we worked on the psychology of those voices. Therein lay forgiveness."

"And what about remembrance, Skyler?" Ms. Martinez asked quietly. "Can we forgive and remember?"

"Well, maybe it takes a certain amount of emotional maturity to remember a trauma, whereas to forget it takes a lot more mental energy. Because you have to hide it. You can't do it forever. I mean, it's not that you want necessarily to broadcast it to the world. It's just that resolving the conflict, over-coming the trauma, is a healthier approach. I will always remember my sister in the kindest of terms. She carried my cross because of the incest. Too many people have borne the cross in my time. Now it's time to pay it forward." Skyler rubbed his brow.

She asked him, "But how do you feel about the whole thing now, as an adult?"

He paused, thinking, then replied, "Well, as an adult, there is the problem of evil, whereas as children, we are supposedly innocent. Evil, I think, presupposes certain themes like abuse, overpowering others for control, hatred, ugliness, and falseness, or lack of truth. I'm just trying these out from what I remember from college." Skyler was using his noggin now, in a free-form kind of manner. They called that kind of feel-good thinking colloquially as "intellectual masturbation" in college.

"There is no doubt that I did an immoral deed on my sister. I think what is important to note is, as the perpetrator, I suffered the voices! Not her! And that's fitting."

"Good point." Ms. Martinez raised a hand. "Do you recall her diagnosis?"

"Major depressive disorder," recalled Skyler.

"Okay, maybe now it makes more sense." She scribbled some notes.

"In another vein, for example, my drug dealer thought he could control me. In fact, he used the drugs as a way of controlling people — everybody, I guess. But I resisted, with my sense of self-respect and mental wits about me. Ultimately, until I broke him down, with a solid blow to his nose. But there was another person, she..." — he stammered as he broke down — "...I cared for her, and out of fear of being hurt, I could not be there for her, even though I displayed as much heroism against that son of a bitch drug dealer to save my own skin."

"Did she save you?" Martinez asked.

"No...yes! She prevented me from going overboard against the dealer's lover. Just enough to avoid spitting on the drug dealer's girlfriend's face and not get really violent against her. Then — by the way, Josie is her name — I had to leave her in the lurch before things got really ugly — before I got blown away with a gun, quite possibly. Whereas I refused to listen to my sister's entreaties, I listened to Josie, in the middle of a manic rage. I listened to her."

Skyler bit his lower lip, then continued, "I want to reach out to her, to Josie, but I don't know how to reach her. I never got her number. And I don't have her email or username. I can't find her on social media. I guess it's too late, huh?"

"Skyler, our time is up, but you told me once, 'Where there's a will. there's a way.' I'm positive about that. If necessary, keep moving on."

At eleven o'clock that morning, Skyler connected via telehealth with Dr. Wilson for their monthly meeting. The conversation started in a rather unoriginal way.

"So, tell me, Skyler, how do you feel?" The doctor put a hand to his mouth.

"Well, I don't really know. I'm not really sure." Skyler cradled his head in both arms.

"Do you think that it's still too early to tell?"

"Hmm. There is one thing that bothers me, Doctor."

"Yes? What is it?"

"I explained to Ms. Martinez what might... excuse me, what is...causing the voice inside my head."

"Yes? It could be an interesting explanation, Skyler." An open smile registered on the doctor's face.

"You won't tell anybody?"

"Not if I want to lose my license. Come on, now. Offer me your 'confession.'" Dr. Wilson gave a winning grin and a chuckle.

"When I was a teenager, I slept with my younger teenage sister." It had taken so long to get it out, but he finally was able to, in a safe place. He even was able to say it in a matter-of-fact way.

"Okay, now I see your point." The grin disappeared from the doctor's face. "Incest is a serious issue, not to be taken lightly. How old were you when the episode happened?"

"I was seventeen, and she was fifteen. "

Dr. Wilson offered his two cents. "Yes, Emily was under my and Ms. Martinez's care. We were aware of what happened. Does that make you at fault for the guilt you feel? Maybe you are wrongly blaming yourself. You two were minors at the time, so to establish you or Emily as the victim or the perpetrator? The deceased cannot offer up a defense, but only you, as one of the living, can 'pay it forward.' Skyler, there is quite a stigma for such a taboo subject, but nothing we cannot talk about behind closed doors. We do not want, nor need, to bring this out in the open. Your secret is safe with me." Dr. Wilson rested his head in one of his own hands.

"I can see you are putting in some hard work into your therapy, and I sense great promise because I have rarely met a patient who put this much effort into their recovery."

"Hmm. Thank you, Doctor."

"Anything else you want to report out?"

"Yes, ah, the voices have gone away and at one

point were replaced by an angelic type of voice that said, 'Your secret is safe with me.' Now that is gone too. The auditory hallucinations have quieted down. Sometimes I sense an urge or a 'tug' in a direction instructing me to do something, but that could be my gut instinct telling me what to do. In any case, it's not distracting."

"Okay, as long as it does not appear to be interfering with your work or personal tasks, then I guess we can let it go. Unless, of course, you want more medication."

"Oh, no, I think a hundred milligrams daily is just fine. Now, as for my moods, you asked me about that..."

"How *are* you feeling in that department, Skyler?"

"I feel...well...I feel quite normal, to be honest with you."

"It seems that the lithium worked well, and maybe the Loxapine helped out in that department. Any side —?"

"And I feel as if the lithium puts a light lid, and bottom, on my emotions. You remember me two months ago, when I would be hot-then-cold, from manic to depressed, or the other way around. I'm sure Ms. Martinez must have picked up on that in our earlier sessions."

"I'm glad to hear that," said Dr. Wilson. "It's usually when we psychiatrists hit upon the right cocktail that we can keep you on it for as long as you need it, with occasional tweaking in dosages here and there. But as I was going to ask, have you noticed any side effects?

"Well, I'm thirsty all the time. I drink a lot of water."

"Yes, lithium is a salt, after all. It is important that you remain hydrated properly. Have a bottle of water around at all times. Otherwise, do you want me to give you something else without the thirst?"

"Oh, no, not at all." A little panicky, Skyler was sure to tell the doctor that, absolutely not, a change was not necessary. "No, I like this medication. I like how it makes me feel, just normal, very stable. I don't know if I have ever felt like this in my life, even before medication."

"Your report-out right now is active and involved. Emotionally, you are quite stable and even-keeled, and you do not exhibit any ongoing symptoms or side effects. Let's keep you on the dosage and type of medications as prescribed. I tell you, Skyler, for me, as your physician, it's like talking to a different person. And that's a good thing."

———

The next day, after a good night's sleep with clean sheets, Skyler woke up around nine and turned on "Shiny Happy People" by the rock band R.E.M. Just then, his phone rang.

Who is this? I don't recognize the number.

He hung up. It rang again. Hung up once more. It rang, this time a third time!

"Hello, who's this?" He felt the old irritability come over in.

Sneaky giggling.

"Okay, now who is this?" He was ready to hang up.

Burst-out laughing.

All right, who the hell is this, dammit? He cursed to himself.

"SKYLER JONES! Is that the way to talk to your buddy, JOSIE?"

Hilarity ensuing.

"Wait...oh my God...who is this?" Recognition swept over him like a storm.

"It's Josie Heller, who did you think?" Haha, gotcha!

"Josie? Oh my God! Do you have any idea how many times I realized I don't have your number? I'm so glad you're not dead!" Skyler opined in a rather obtuse manner.

A welcome blast from the past! He turned down the music on his laptop, lay on his back on his bed, and balanced his phone on his racing heart.

She told him, "You really flipped out back last month. It was very impressive. You shut them down right where it hurts the most, in their faces! Haha!"

"You know, I followed your instructions not to mess up Jeanne's mug. I'm sorry if I scared you. I'm serious. None of that was meant for you to witness. I didn't want you to see that. But maybe it was for the best that you did." He started to get all weepy.

Christ, I'm losing it in front of her!

"Hey, Skyler. Trust me, I get it. My brother is bipolar. Did you know that? I've seen his outbursts many times before. It was just getting all hairy back there, with Reggie sinking his dragon talons into Jeanne, humiliating you, and threatening me!"

She had more to say. "By the way, I gave my own outburst to Jeanne and Reggie. I went over there the next day and told them I couldn't find you, that you had taken off somewhere. I gave Jeanne an earful. She wasn't looking good. Her face was as white as a sheet, and she didn't have that same old hot-girl allure either. She looked very anxious and very scared. I told her, to her contorted face, that she was a dirty, disease-infested bitch! She started to cry! She couldn't believe that her dearest 'friend' would say something like that to her. It just goes to show how weak she is. Now she has no power over anybody, including over Reggie."

"You didn't, did you?"

"Ha, you better believe it! And Reggie still looked like he had spray-painted his face red. I screamed at him, 'Reggie, you are a low-life scumbag greaseball piece of shit drug dealer!'"

"Wow, Josie. Honestly, honey, you have more courage than I do."

"Yeah, that's enough for a while, right? But I told Reggie, 'If you want to do me a big favor and not want me to rat you out to the police, you'll give me Skyler's number.'"

"So that's how you found me."

"But after that was when I got the hell out of there. That reminds me, you forgot your fleece pullover. I took it with me after you left and hoped to catch you before you took off too far."

"I was wondering why I felt so cold when I got out of there. Can you hold onto it for me for a little while?"

"Sure! But seriously, Sky, we can't hang out with that crew anymore. And I'm giving up on pot. I don't like how it makes me feel — dizzy, out of control, paranoid. Lots of bad memories. And you know I never did those powders, right? You saw me. Or rather, you didn't see me. I was just watching out for Jeanne the whole time so that she wouldn't go out with Reggie. But she's lost — completely gone. They're definitely sleeping with each other. And I can't be around Reggie either. It's over. Just nicotine and caffeine for me."

"Geez, that's brilliant, Josie! If I can take a page from your book, I think I should only do those two. That helps my recovery from mental illness and abstinence from drugs."

"Say, if you're on the same page with those, how would you feel about getting together for coffee and cigarettes and conversation? You know, sometime soon? Sometime this morning?"

"Hmm..." Skyler deliberated. "You mean, with me?"

"Yeah, you, silly! What did you think, a reunion with Reggie and Jeanne?" She laughed at this dunce.

"No, of course not. I'll bring the Camel Lights? We both like that."

"You got it. And I'll get the Peet's Coffee? We both dig that."

"Sure thing. But hey, I don't have a ride anymore."

"How about if I pick you up?"

"Sure, but when will we get together? I'm worried it will cut into our schedules."

"What, you got something to do right now? What, you got a plane to catch?"

Peals of laughter emanated through the radio waves.

"No, it's not that. I just don't want you getting mixed up in the wrong kind of company."

She snorted, "You really are crazy, you know that? Come on. Let's do it today."

"Okay, but I have a question for you. Where have you been this past month? Did you have my number but waited, you know, hesitated to call me? Were you not sure of me?"

"Okay, Skyler, I'll answer your question, straight up. I decided to move from North Hollywood to East Hollywood. I wanted to be on the other side of the mountains and out of the Valley. I wanted to be closer to the action. And besides, East Hollywood is more my speed with all the young single people all over the place. It took a few weeks and change to lug all my stuff to over here and get all situated, you know."

Skyler rolled over on his side. "Okay, now I can understand better why the radio silence. You just seemed to fall off the face of the earth. Besides, I didn't have your number, so I just couldn't call you back."

"Plus, you should know, Sky, that I'm careful when it comes to guys. I am friendly to every guy I meet, but I have trust issues. And maybe you do too. Let's be honest. I thought about it a lot. I think we both have skeletons in our closet. I wanted to give you space for about a month's time and then see what happened when I contacted you. I saw you at your worst back then. I promised myself I wouldn't try to reach you until after Christmas. That's all."

"You want to know something? My birthday is

on Christmas." He giggled like a little schoolgirl out of an abundance of happiness.

"Okay, so now do you see? It worked out. Now, can you make it at ten? In less than an hour?" She stood up, raring to go to her car.

"I'm living with my Uncle Frank and Aunt Nancy. You know their address?"

She knows everything, I guess.

"Yeah, I do. Five hundred Winding Road Terrace, right?"

What? She does *know everything!*

"Wait, how do you know that?" Skyler knit his eyebrows.

"Hey, I'm full of surprises. Cool. Is it a deal?"

He exhaled a huge gust of air. "Yeah, it's a deal!" The old-time feeling of something about to happen — the action — came to him.

"Okay, see you soon!"

Skyler looked down, sad to end the conversation. "See you!"

"Oh, and, uh, you're my hero, Sky. You rescued me." She said it willingly, wryly, wistfully.

"Yeah? Why?" He chortled. "You didn't know me until two months ago. And for the first month, I was a party-hardy druggie. Then I disappeared for a month. And by the way, I have some stories. So how could I possibly be a perfectly sober addict and a fully recovered nut job after all that?"

"Ha! I know! Let me jog your memory: CAMCORDER!"

"Camcorder? What camcorder? What's going on?" Then it dawned on him. "Oh, THAT camcorder!" Now it was coming to him. "Hold on, wait! You have it? Like...in your possession?"

"I sure do! Just before you began raising hell — destroying private property, punching drug dealers, spitting on bitches — I turned the thing on and started recording. I even caught Reggie and Jeanne afterward while they were yelling and screaming bloody murder in the bathroom. They tried to humiliate you and me, but the evidence truly shows that they were the ones who were humiliated. Anyhow, I ran out of there with both Reggie's camcorder and your pullover." She giggled between gasps of air.

That explained the lump he felt with his arm when Josie went to restrain him. Instead, she had been holding the camcorder in her right hand! And he had thought it was a gun.

"You rescued me, Skyler. You rescued me from Jeanne, who ruined my friendship and forced me to end it. You rescued me from Reggie, who baited me with drugs and showed no respect. No one was willing to fight for me, to go to bat for me. But you had my back. And you did it when you were completely hammered, with all the adversity, danger and weakness I saw just weighing, weighing, weighing you down. You risked your life to get me out of that sticky situation, and just as importantly, you listened when I asked you to cool off. You're not crazy. You're my hero. You are my knight in shining armor, Skyler Jones. Get it now?" It was an imploring tone of voice that she was using on him, like a last-ditch attempt to bring him onboard to her side.

Skyler could count on one hand the times he had cried in his whole adult life: when he had lost his family, when he slept in his BMW in fetal position, when he dealt with his mental health diagnosis, when he battled his drug addiction, and when he had just voiced concern over Josie witnessing his violent streak. Now, he felt...happy? He had felt that way the night before when he accompanied Uncle Frank on the Steinway grand to "Amazing Grace" for an intimate audience of one, Aunt Nancy. And earlier this morning, the music of R.E.M.'s "Shiny Happy People" had burst through, bathing Skyler in happy airwaves. And now, at this moment, he badly needed — and badly wanted — to make it a two-street.

As if he had never fully trusted another person until now,

As if he had never believed in saying it until the present,

As if he had never cared for another, until in the moment.

At last, he told her, "And you are my lady, Josie Heller, whose honor and life I will defend and protect. I am your champion!" Unhesitatingly. Unconditionally. Unreservedly.

Click.

As he got ready, Skyler waited for ten...

▭

ACKNOWLEDGMENTS

I would like to thank author and colleague Gerald Everett Jones, editor, and La Puerta Productions, for his editorial comments and for carrying the editorial process to its logical conclusion. I would also like to thank Robin Quinn, editor, and Quinn's Word for Word, for her helpful comments on previous versions of the manuscript.

I will share my motivations: mental illness and drug addiction are on the rise in American society—and not merely among the homeless and jail populations. Dual diagnosis, also known as co-occuring disorder, is ravaging college campuses, and if it is there, it may have migrated to high schools, and perhaps further down. The tide seems irresistible.

But my book about this lived experience, written with hope for the future, and read with high purpose, could turn things around, one reader at a time.

The answer to this social scourge is not distressingly far, but tantalizingly close, if we only have the courage to look for it in ourselves.

ABOUT THE AUTHOR

Jason W Park, PhD was born in Lawrence, KS, and raised in Pittsburgh, PA. He has called Los Angeles his home since 1997. Dr. Park earned his AB with honors in philosophy from Harvard and his PhD in strategic management from the University of Pittsburgh. These academic experiences influence his writing style.

Jason played the piano at Carnegie Hall in a concert for talented youth. He was also a jazz DJ for the college radio station. These aesthetic experiences grace his approach to literary material.

ABOUT THE AUTHOR

ALSO BY JASON W PARK, PhD

JASONJJPARK.COM

The Australian Wager: A True Short Story

The Piano Is Your B.F.F. Kindle Edition

Full Moon Chess With A Romanian Kindle Edition

Bliss + Blues = Bipolar: A Memoir of My Ups and Downs
Living with Bipolar Disorder

Late Night Visit from the Boys and Girl in Blue: A Short
Story

J.J. MAGIK
—— publishing ——

www.ingramcontent.com/pod-product-compliance
Lightning Source LLC
Chambersburg PA
CBHW050845180626
46814CB00007B/2633